THE CHEF'S CHOICE

KRISTIN HARDY

SPECIAL EDITION

Published by Silhouette Books

America's Publisher of Contemporary Romance

SILHOUETTE BOOKS

ISBN-13: 978-0-373-24919-0
ISBN-10:   0-373-24919-5

THE CHEF'S CHOICE

Visit Silhouette Books at www.eHarlequin.com

Printed in U.S.A.

KRISTIN HARDY

has always wanted to write, and started her first novel while still in grade school. Although she became a laser engineer by training, she never gave up her dream of being an author. In 2002, her first completed manuscript, *My Sexiest Mistake,* debuted in Harlequin's Blaze line; it was subsequently made into a movie by the Oxygen network. Kristin lives in New Hampshire with her husband and collaborator. Check out her Web site at www.kristinhardy.com.

Acknowledgments

Thanks go to Chef Jonathan Cartwright
and his staff at the White Barn Inn,
for giving me a window into their world,
to Eric Lusty at the Dockside Guest Quarters,
for taking me behind the scenes
and Joe DeSalazar, food blogger extraordinaire
(www.blog.foodienyc.com), for the ramps.

Dedication

To Shannon, for the dreams,
to Teresa, for everything
to Gail and Charles (may he live forever)
for not hunting me down and strangling me
and, of course, to Stephen,
who understands the true secret ingredient

Chapter One

"Mind the front desk? Me?" Cady McBain looked up from where she was planting a flowering kale to stare at her mother plaintively.

"Only a few hours. Just until your father and I get back from Portland," Amanda McBain added hastily.

Cady almost smiled. McBains had run the Compass Rose Guest Quarters for four generations. For her parents and even her brother and sister before they'd moved away, tending to guests at the Maine inn was second nature, effortless.

For Cady, it was usually excruciating.

There were times she was sure there'd been a mix-up at the hospital when she was a baby. Give her a hedge to trim or pansies to plant, and she'd go at it with gusto. She kept the grounds of the Compass Rose impeccable, from the flower beds to the trees to the emerald back lawn that ran down to the lapping waters of tiny Grace Harbor. Cady could make sense of plants. She understood them, they were predictable.

She couldn't make heads or tails of people.

It wasn't that she didn't try—although dealing with guests was right up there with root canals on her list of fun things to do. Somehow, though, she always said or did the wrong thing.

"Where's Lynne?" she asked now, thinking of the brisk, efficient woman who worked as their desk clerk.

"She called in sick but we can't reschedule your father's appointment."

"Didn't Dad go to the doctor last week?" Cady rose, brushing the dirt off her hands.

"He did, but Dr. Belt wanted him to have some tests."

"Tests?" She frowned. "What kind of tests?"

"You'll find out after you turn fifty," Ian McBain said darkly as he walked up behind them. "Suffice it to say you'll never look at fruit juice the same way again. Anyway, it's all a waste of time. I'm as healthy as a horse."

"And we want to keep you that way." Cady smoothed his hair where the morning breeze off the water had ruffled it. "Go to your appointment."

"I hope we're not messing up your schedule too much," her mother said.

Cady shrugged. "I was planning to work the grounds all day, anyway. I can keep an eye on the place." She didn't add that she'd anticipated spending at least half of it in the gleaming greenhouse she'd put up earlier that spring at the back of the property, the heated greenhouse where bedding plants for her fledgling landscaping business were already stretching their heads aboveground.

Ian looked from Cady to Amanda. "You're leaving her in charge?"

Amanda raised a brow. "You have a better idea?"

"Cancel my appointment?" he offered hopefully.

"Nice try." She turned toward the house.

"You're not going to run off all our guests, are you?" Ian gave Cady an uneasy look. "We do actually need to make some money. That new roof isn't going to pay for itself, you know."

"Leave it to me, Daddio," she soothed. "I'll take care of everything."

"Why do I get nervous when you say that?" he asked, but he slung an arm around her shoulders as they walked up the steps to the back deck of the inn.

The Compass Rose Guest Quarters had been built in 1911 to provide rooms for the clientele of her great-great-grandfather Archie McBain's main business, the marina next door. For four generations, the sprawling white clapboard inn had perched at the edge of Grace Harbor. The original neo-Colonial style had long since been obscured by almost a century's worth of additions. Now, the building stretched out in all directions, rising three stories to a roofline festooned with dormer windows and red brick chimneys. It should have been a fright, but wrapped by a broad porch and softened by rhododendrons the height of a man, it somehow managed to look warm and friendly and welcoming.

Family lore held that it had been Archie's wife, Jenny, who'd planted the maple that spread its branches over the little spit of land at the back, and Donal's wife, Manya, who'd added the white gazebo. Donal's son, Malcolm—Cady's grandfather—had contributed the quartet of four-room guest-houses that clustered around the main inn. There, guests who wanted more privacy could enjoy their own decks overlooking the harbor.

White sailboats still bobbed at the docks of the Grace Harbor marina next door, but it was owned these days by Cady's uncle Lenny and run by her cousin Tucker. She saw Tucker on the docks, dark and lanky, and raised an arm to acknowledge his wave before they stepped inside.

"Now, we've only got three rooms full at present," Amanda told her, crossing the lobby to the Dutch door that served as the inn's front desk. "Six guests."

Cady didn't miss the frown that flickered over her father's face. In early May, the Maine tourist season was weeks away, but they still should have had at least double the number of occupied rooms. Especially with the new roof, her parents needed every penny they could get.

The clank of spoons on china had Cady glancing down the hall off the lobby in the direction of the morning room. "What about breakfast? Where are you at there?"

"Just started," Amanda said. "One couple is eating, the rest are still in their rooms. Everything's set up, though. All you need to do is keep an eye on things, stock up whatever needs it. Make nice, clean up afterward. You know the drill."

"For about the past twenty-seven years," Cady agreed.

"Fresh," her mother said.

Cady's lips twitched. "This is a surprise?"

"They're a pretty easy bunch," Amanda continued, ignoring her. "With any luck, things will be quiet while we're gone."

Ian's snort sounded suspiciously like a smothered laugh. It was an inn. Things were never quiet, Cady knew, unless it was empty, and often not even then. Hope could spring eternal, though.

"Anyone coming in today?" she asked.

"One guest. He's not due until after we get back."

"Where's his registration, just in case?"

"His paperwork and keys are right here." Amanda opened the Dutch door and went into the tiny office and kitchenette behind to pull an envelope from a wicker organizer. "You shouldn't have to deal with him, though."

"Perish the thought," Ian muttered.

Amanda elbowed him. "Hush, you. She'll do fine. Won't you, Cady?"

"I'll be the milk of human kindness," she promised, tongue firmly in cheek. "Now get going or you're going to hit traffic."

She followed them outside and watched them walk toward the parking lot, hand in hand, like always. Since she'd been a child, the two constants in her life had been the inn and her parents' quiet love for each other. For an instant, she felt a tug of wistfulness. She'd always assumed that someday she'd find a love like that, at least until she'd hit high school and discovered that what guys wanted were curvy, blond cheerleader types with Pepsodent smiles, not opinionated, auburn-haired tomboys.

Well, she was who she was, for better or worse. The day she'd given up looking for romance with a good-looking charmer had been the day she'd finally started to get comfortable in her own skin. And at twenty-seven she wasn't about to change for anyone.

She washed her hands and tied on an apron. Even though the Compass Rose boasted a separate restaurant, breakfast had always been in the morning room of the main building. Despite the fact that the inn's restaurant employed a half-dozen cooks, responsibility for breakfast had always fallen on Amanda and Ian and the front desk staff.

And on that particular day, the front desk staff was Cady.

She sighed. It wasn't that she couldn't be polite, exactly, it was just that she had strong opinions. And maybe her patience was a teensy bit limited. Okay, maybe a lot limited. Her father, now, he could be interested in just about anyone for as long as they wanted to chat.

Cady tried—sort of—but somehow it never worked. The problem was her face. It always showed exactly what she was thinking, and if she was thinking that the person she was talking with was a bore or a fool, well…

It could be a problem.

Shaking her head, she pasted a smile firmly across her

face and walked into the morning room to begin refilling the stocks of coffee, hot water, muffins and fruit. One pair of the missing guests had arrived and were tucking in with gusto. A little too much gusto, she realized—the orange juice pitcher was nearly empty. Unfortunately, so was the carton in the little refrigerator tucked back in the office.

Perfect. An hour left to run on breakfast, one pair of guests still to arrive and her with no orange juice. Time to get resourceful, she thought, grabbing the carton and hurrying out the door.

Outside, the air smelled of the sea and the pines that grew up around the cedar-shingled restaurant building. Cady slipped stealthily through the back door to the pantry and dishwashing area, heading toward the walk-in refrigerator. She'd just liberate a little juice, enough to refill, that was all.

"Don't you be tracking dirt on my clean floor," a voice said.

Cady jumped and looked guiltily through the doorway to the kitchen. "Roman, what are you doing here?"

"Writing my memoirs." The young, mocha-skinned sous chef glanced over from where he was mincing onions. "There's nothing to eat here. Go over to the breakfast room if you want food."

"That's where I just came from. I'm on desk duty."

He stared. "You?"

Cady rolled her eyes. "Yes, me. Lynne's sick, Mom and Dad are out for the morning. I'm pitching in. I can do it, you know."

"Your parents gotta get some more help." He resumed chopping, shaking his head.

"The way I hear it, you're the one who needs more help," she countered as she ducked into the little passage that led to the walk-in.

The restaurant's head chef, Nathan Eberhardt, had moved on three weeks before, leaving Roman to run things in his stead. While Roman was both a talented line cook and a tireless worker, he was barely twenty-three. He hadn't anything like enough experience to be suddenly managing the complicated dance of running a kitchen. To his credit, that hadn't stopped him. He'd kept things going, mostly by dint of practically living at the restaurant.

"You've got assistants for prep," she called over her shoulder. "You're running the joint, Roman. Delegate. Either that or you're going to drown in it."

"Still breathing air, last time I checked," he grunted. "And anyway, I might—wait a minute, what's that noise?" He came around the corner in his chef's whites. "What the heck do you think you're doing?"

"Just getting some orange juice for breakfast." Cady hastily stepped out of the icy refrigerator.

"Oh, no, you're not. Get your own."

"It's not for me, it's for the breakfast bar. Come on, it's just a little juice," she wheedled.

"I got twenty pounds of salmon to marinate. No such thing as a little orange juice." He shook his knife at her.

"I brought you tomatoes yesterday," she protested.

"Don't think that gets you off the hook." For a big guy, he moved fast.

Lucky she was small and faster. "Think of the headlines. Juicing Chef Offs Plucky Desk Clerk." Cady made a break for the door. "What will Malika do while you're in jail?"

"Buy her own orange juice, I hope," Roman growled, but she saw his grin before she escaped out the door.

She'd say this for working the desk: the time went quickly. She'd blinked once, maybe twice, and it was going on one in the afternoon. Of course, time had a way of flying when you were lurching from crisis to crisis.

Every time the door opened, it seemed, it heralded another person with a problem or question or emergency for her. As always, living a bit of her parents' life only increased her respect for them. Roman was right; they needed more help, whether they could afford it or not. A few hours into one of their days and already she was worn-out.

She'd cleaned up breakfast dishes, folded bedspreads and sheets in the laundry, vacuumed the lobby, baked scones for afternoon tea. She'd handed out directions, jumped the car of a guest who'd left her dome light on all night and calmed the hysterics of a maid who'd found a mouse in the linen closet. Smiling, always smiling, even talking to the guest who'd plugged his toilet trying to flush a washcloth.

A washcloth.

What was it about people in hotels? she wondered for the thousandth time as she hurried back to the office behind the reception area to call the plumber. They did things that they would never do at home. What kind of ninny put a washcloth down a toilet? And now, here she was with another maintenance bill to further stretch the inn's budget, already strained to its breaking point.

Like her patience.

The door jingled again and she flinched.

"Anybody home?" A man's voice carried in through the open top of the Dutch door. Cady could hear his boot heels thud on the lobby floor with each step. Not one of the staff. It didn't sound like one of the guests she'd packed off to go shopping in Freeport or Kennebunkport, either, which probably meant that it was the day's arrival. Perfect. The fact that check-in was clearly listed as 3:00 p.m. never stopped guests from showing up an hour or two early and blithely expecting to be shown to their rooms, whether the maids had finished their cleaning rounds or not.

"Hello?"

"Just a minute." Suppressing the urge to snap, Cady walked to the opening. "What do you—"

And her voice died in her throat.

His was the face of a sixteenth-century libertine. Lean and angular, with razor-sharp cheekbones, it was a face that knew pleasure. She could imagine him dueling at dawn or seducing high-born ladies. She could imagine him slashing paint over canvas in an artist's garret or bending over a keyboard, pounding out impassioned blues in a smoky, late-night club.

His dark, straight brows matched the wavy hair that flowed to his shoulders. He hadn't bothered to shave that morning and the shadow of a beard ran along the bottom of his face like the artful shading of a charcoal sketch, drawing attention to the line of jaw, the strong chin, framing his mouth.

His mouth.

Temptation and mischief, fascination and promise. It was the kind of mouth that offered laughter, the kind of mouth that offered an invitation to decadence.

And delicious, lingering kisses.

Sudden color flooded her cheeks. Look at her, standing there staring at him like an idiot.

Get it together, Cady.

She cleared her throat. "Welcome to the Compass Rose. Are you here to check in?"

"Kind of. I'm looking for Amanda or Ian McBain."

"They're not around just now, I'm afraid. I'd be happy to help you, though."

The corner of his mouth curved up a bit. "My good luck."

It was said with the casual ease of a guy who turned every woman he met into putty, the kind of guy who charmed as second nature. Her eyes narrowed. She wasn't big on good-looking guys in general, and she was in no mood to be charmed, not after the morning she'd had. "Your room's probably not ready this early, but I'll check with housekeeping." When she got around to it. "Here's your paperwork, anyway. It's Donnelly, right? Scott Donnelly?"

"Hurst," he corrected. "Damon Hurst."

"Welcome to the Compass Rose Guest Quarters, Mr.—" Cady stopped. Stared at him blankly. "Damon Hurst?" she repeated. "*The* Damon Hurst?"

"The same."

She saw it now—the famous cheekbones, the Renaissance hair, the face that had graced a hundred magazine covers.

And a thousand tabloid stories over his half decade of infamy.

Damon Hurst, the enfant terrible of the Cooking Channel, the charismatic star who'd sent the upstart network soaring against its entrenched rival before he'd flamed out the year before. Known more for his baroque personal life and volatile kitchen persona than for his undeniably brilliant cuisine, he'd been the subject of speculation, rumors, spite and stories too outrageous to be believed.

Except that they were true.

Cady cleared her throat. "Yes, well, welcome to the Compass Rose, Mr. Hurst," she said. "It'll take a little time to get a room put together for you but we do have a vacancy. If you'll just fill out the registration form, please?" She put the paper on the little counter that topped the lower half of the door.

"I'm not checking in."

Cady frowned. "I'm not sure I understand."

"The restaurant."

"Ah. I see." She hadn't realized that the Sextant, the Compass Rose's restaurant, had a reputation that stretched all the way to Manhattan. Then again, with his shows very publicly canceled and his restaurant doors shuttered, maybe Damon Hurst had little else to do than run around obscure eateries in Maine. She dredged up a faint smile. "The Sextant is just across the parking lot. I believe they're still serving lunch."

"I'm not here for lunch, either," he said. He was laughing at her, she realized, and she felt her face flame.

"If you're hoping for a tour of the restaurant, I think you're out of luck." Even she could hear the tartness in her voice.

"We're shorthanded and I doubt our chef has any interest in letting you go traipsing around his kitchen."

"My kitchen, now," Hurst corrected. "I guess you haven't heard. I'm the new chef."

Chapter Two

He was used to having a strong effect on women. Attraction, arousal, jealousy, anger.

Rarely horror.

"Our new chef?" She stared at him, dismay writ large on her features, as though he were a fry cook from some seaside clam shack, Damon thought in irritation.

"The restaurant's new chef," he corrected. And tried not to wonder yet again what the hell he was doing.

"You want to get your life back in gear?" his mentor, legendary chef Paul Descour, had demanded over port at his landmark Manhattan restaurant, Lyon. "Make a fresh start. Go away from here. Find a good restaurant with room to grow and turn it into something. Remind yourself that you're still a chef, instead of a…" He'd waved at the air in disgust and dismissal.

Dismissing what? A top-rated cooking show four years

running? A bestselling cookbook? A *Michelin*-starred restaurant, Pommes de Terre, deemed the best of Manhattan by the *Times?*

And a very public firing, the voice in Damon's head reminded him. A restaurant backer who'd walked away from those Michelin stars and left him hanging. The wreckage of a dozen friendships that littered the wake of his career. The hundred meaningless liaisons that had been poor substitutes.

And the morning he'd woken and looked back at himself in the mirror, knowing there needed to be more.

"You're our new chef?" the feisty-looking redhead before him repeated incredulously. "I don't believe it. This is a family business. I can't imagine they'd do something so…so…"

"So?" he prompted, letting the annoyance show. He topped her by more than a head but she stared back at him, not giving an inch. It was the eyes that did it, a hazel that wasn't quite green, wasn't quite brown, eyes that stared back at him unimpressed, daring him to justify himself.

He didn't need to justify himself to anyone.

Descour and his big ideas. Nathan Eberhardt, the new sous chef at Lyon, had left the Sextant minus an executive chef. The perfect opportunity, Paul had said. Sure. The perfect opportunity to come up to the sticks and get dissed at the front desk by some clerk in a dirt-smudged work shirt and shaggy hair.

Find a good restaurant with room to grow and turn it into something.

"Look, whether you believe it or not, it's happening," he said shortly. "They probably just forgot to tell you." Or didn't bother, he thought, diagnosing her as a troublemaker on sight.

"Oh, trust me, they didn't forget." Temper snapped in her eyes. "So let me get this straight. You're Nathan's replacement?"

"Looks that way," he agreed. "And you are?"

"Cady McBain. Amanda and Ian are my parents."

"Ah." He raised his eyebrows.

"What's that supposed to mean?"

She was ticked because she'd been blindsided. "I guess they forgot to run it by you."

"I don't think that's any of your business."

"Maybe not," he said, "but it's bugging you."

She scowled at him. "Does Roman know?"

"Roman?"

"You have met Roman, right? Your sous chef?"

"Oh, right." He shrugged. "I haven't met any of the staff yet. I was down in New York." None of her business that he'd taken the job sight unseen, and happy to get it. He hadn't been foolish, exactly, with the money he'd made. At least not all of it. The problem was, you couldn't eat a TriBeCa loft or a Le Corbusier sofa. For form's sake, he'd taken a few days to think over Amanda and Ian McBain's telephone offer, but he'd already begun making arrangements to be gone for however long it took to fight his way back.

The hazel eyes were narrowed at him. She might have had lashes that a few of his model-actress ex-bedmates would have killed for, but they did nothing to soften that stare. "Listen to me. Roman Bennett is the most talented, hard-working line cook you'll ever meet. He's been killing himself twenty hours a day since Nathan left to hold this place together. You give him a hard time, you'll answer to me."

His lips twitched; he couldn't help it.

She glowered. "Don't laugh at me."

It took all he had not to. Here she was, a head shorter than he was and she was threatening him. And she was dead serious, he realized, the smile fading.

"I'm not a jackass," he said.

"You'll pardon me if I prefer to wait and see on that one."

The snap in her words stung. Now it was his turn to step a bit closer. "Wait and see about what?"

"Whether you live up to your reputation."

Taking his time, keeping control of the irritation, he leaned down to rest his elbows on the counter so that they were eye to eye, lip to lip. She smelled faintly of apples. And he could see her decide not to budge. "It's a good thing we'll have lots of time, then."

For a minute, neither moved. And he couldn't help wondering what she would do if he shifted just a bit closer, tasted that mouth of hers while it was open and soft with surprise. He saw her shoulders rise slightly as she took a breath, saw those hazel eyes darken to caramel brown.

And flicker with alarm.

She did move then, abruptly. "Stop playing games." Her voice was sharp.

"Stop playing hardnose."

"I'm not playing anything."

"Really?" He watched the pulse beat in her throat. "This could get interesting."

Just then, the door behind him jingled. "We're back," a voice announced from the door and he turned to see a woman with Cady's eyes walking in.

He could almost hear Cady's sigh of relief. "This has been fun, but here are my parents. I guess it's time for you to finally meet your staff."

"I guess you're right," Damon said. "See you around."

"Not if I see you first."

"Do you have any idea what you've taken on here?" Cady stared at her parents across their kitchen.

"Of course," Amanda said pleasantly, glancing over her shoulder as she stood at the counter with bread and cold cuts. "Do you want me to make you a sandwich, too?"

"No thanks," Cady muttered.

"You can give me hers," Ian said cheerfully. "There's nothing like fasting for a couple of days to make a guy appreciate food."

"You're changing the subject," Cady returned, although a

sandwich was starting to sound increasingly good for someone who'd skipped lunch. "Why Damon Hurst, of all people?
There have to be tons of qualified cooks out there."

"Cooks, maybe, but not chefs, and not as many as you'd
think. At least not who'd move up to Grace Harbor."

Okay, so a tiny tourist town, even one an hour from
Portland, wasn't for everyone. Still... "There has to be
someone. Why Hurst? Why him, of all people?"

He'd leaned in and stared at her with those eyes and she'd
almost forgotten how to breathe. *This could get interesting.*
Just thinking of it made her furious.

Just thinking of it made her shiver.

"We hired him because he was recommended by Nathan,
for one thing," her father said, pulling a bowl of potato chips
toward himself.

Cady blinked. "Nathan knows him?"

"Well, the chef Nathan works for now does. He told
Nathan, Nathan told us."

"He said he hadn't even been here. What, he couldn't even
be bothered to come interview? He made you go there?"

Her father coughed. "Not exactly."

"You took him on sight unseen?" she asked incredulously.

"We took him on recommendation. We talked to him by
phone, several times. We'd seen him cook on *Chef's Challenge,* where he has a winning record, I might add. What
more did we need to know?"

"I don't know, chemistry? See if it feels right?"

"Chemistry?" Ian repeated in amusement. "We don't want
a date, we want a chef. I don't see the problem. He needs a
job and he can give us what we need, which is visibility."

"Or notoriety."

"You know what they say. There's no such thing as bad
publicity," Amanda put in mildly as she set the sandwiches
down on the table and sat.

"Mom, you know the stories. I mean, he used to throw customers out of his restaurant, for God's sakes. He gave one of his chefs a black eye. Do you want that happening at the Sextant?"

"Of course not. But he says that's over. He wants to build something here."

"Sure, until he finds something bigger and better and walks out on his contract." There was a short silence while her parents suddenly became very interested in their napkins. "You do have him under contract, don't you?" Cady asked with dawning dismay.

Ian met her eyes. "We thought about it but we decided it was smarter not to. A contract is a double-edged sword, you know. This way if he doesn't work out, we can walk away."

"You do admit there's a chance of that, then?"

"Of course we do," Ian said impatiently. "It's a calculated risk."

"I agree with the risk part."

"No matter what, we'll get a lot of exposure from him. People know Damon Hurst. They'll want to know why he's here. They'll come to see if he's still got the magic. I mean, think of it, even you've heard of him and you barely pick up a paper or turn on the TV."

"Cable's too expensive," she muttered, moving to sit at the table with them.

"Our occupancy is down. It *has* been for the past two years. We need to get publicity and we can't afford ads right now." Ian picked up his sandwich. "Hurst's our answer. We send out a few press releases, maybe get a review or two in the papers or magazines."

And start a media feeding frenzy. "That publicity's not going to be worth much if your line staff quits and your diners start staying away."

"I think that's unlikely."

"I don't trust him." Cady reached out for a chip. "Why

would a guy like him come all the way up here to work? You know the stories—he dates fashion models and pop tarts. I can't imagine Grace Harbor's going to thrill him."

"Maybe he's grown up. It can happen, you know." Amanda gave her a bland look.

"All right, all right, I get the point," Cady grumbled. "But he's got to be costing you a fortune."

"Not as much as you'd think. We've caught him at a good time. And he's got big plans for the Sextant."

"For now, anyway." Then again, as much as she desperately wanted her parents' inn to succeed, Damon Hurst couldn't be gone soon enough for her peace of mind.

"We need him, Cady." For once, there was no humor in her father's voice. "We're in a deep hole. We need all the bounce we can get from him and if you don't trust him you'd better hope that you're wrong and Nathan and Descour are right. We need you to do everything you possibly can to make this work."

"But—"

"We're not asking you to marry the man, just keep a civil tongue in your head," Ian shot back, temporarily silencing her. "If you can't do that much, then just stay away."

Cady looked at them both and sighed. "Of course I'll help however I can. I think you're both nuts but if Damon Hurst is what you want, Damon Hurst is what you'll get. God help you," she added.

"Tell me again why having a gorgeous man who's a fabulous chef and a celebrity working at your parents' restaurant is a bad thing?" Cady's best friend since childhood, Tania Martin, peered at her from the other end of the couch.

Cady scowled and scooped up some sesame chicken from one of the myriad takeout containers that littered the crates-and-boards combination that could charitably be called her coffee table. It was their weekly movie/gossip/junk food night, or at least Tania's.

Cady believed in eating junk food as often as possible.

In a crowded room, nobody would ever have picked the two of them to be friends. Unlike tomboy Cady, who pretty well lived in jeans and a T-shirt, Tania kept on the cutting edge of hip with her black spiky hair and tinkling silver jewelry and her scarlet—or sometimes blue—nails and lips. They'd known each other since second grade and were as close as sisters.

"Why is Damon Hurst a bad thing?" Cady repeated, sprinkling soy sauce over her chicken with a free hand. "He's irresponsible. He's temperamental. He got fired from his TV show *and* from his restaurant for not taking care of business. He makes scenes. You, of all people, should know because you're the one who told me about all of it."

"Besides all that." Tania crunched into an egg roll.

"Besides…Tania, the guy got caught boinking one of his customers in his office—by the woman's husband. You want to tell me again how you think him being here could in any way be a *good* idea?"

"Okay, so he has some rough edges," Tania allowed, forking up some fried rice. "Anyway, that boinking story was from years ago. Maybe he's past it by now."

"God help us if he's not." Cady squeezed a dollop of hot mustard out of its packet and swabbed her egg roll in it.

Tania watched her a minute. "Do you know you've probably burned off every taste bud you were ever born with by now?" she asked as Cady tore open a second packet. "How can you eat that stuff?"

"Puts hair on your chest." Cady bit into the egg roll with a little hum of pleasure.

"Just what I've always wanted. Anyway, back to Damon Hurst—and I expect an introduction to him at the first possible moment, by the way—what are you going to do?"

Cady aimed the remote at her DVD player moodily. "Not much I can do. Mom and Dad seem to think he's the answer to their problems."

"And you don't agree. You know you're only prejudiced against him because he's good-looking."

"I'm prejudiced against him because he's trouble. He's one of those guys who thinks he can get anything he wants."

"Can he?" Tania asked curiously.

"Watch the movie."

"It's just previews." Tania turned to face her. "This is much more interesting. Come on, what's he really like?"

What was he really like? "A charmer, like it's second nature. He knows exactly what to say and how to say it. He's got this way of looking at you so that even when you're ready to strangle him all you can do is just stand there staring up at him like an idiot."

Tania became very still. "'You' like hypothetical or 'you' like you?" she asked carefully.

"Do I look like an idiot?"

"I'll pass on answering that just now."

"He's so cocky, he thinks he's God's gift and he can get you to do whatever he wants you to. 'This could get interesting,' my ass," Cady burst out in frustration. She sprang up from the couch and began pacing.

Tania just watched. "You're getting awfully excited about a guy you hardly know."

"It doesn't take long with him. I mean, he leans in and gets right in my face, deliberately, when he *knows* I'm pissed about him. And he does that thing with his eyes—"

"What thing with his eyes?"

"Like he wants to eat you up," she responded, moving restlessly to the window. "Like you're the only person in the world. And he makes you want to believe it." It was irritating. Beyond irritating, infuriating.

"Let's go back to the 'eat you up' part," Tania ordered. "You mean he tried to kiss you?"

Cady stopped and flopped back down on the couch. "Give me some credit, will you? I would have stopped that one way before it ever happened."

"Why?"

"Why?" she repeated.

Tania forked up a dumpling. "You ask me, you could use kissing. How long has it been, anyway?"

"You know how long it's been." Cady took a drink of her Coke. "Since Ed Shaw."

Tania stared. "Ed Shaw was what, three years ago? Cady, sweetie, you've got to get out more."

"Maybe I don't want to," she retorted. "I mean, it's fine for you. You're gorgeous, you've always got guys after you. It doesn't work that way for me."

"That's because you scare 'em off with that mouth of yours."

"Maybe I want to scare them off. Maybe I just don't want to deal with it." She didn't want the nerves, didn't like the anticipation, despised that feeling of having it suddenly matter whether some guy called or not. And having no control over whether or not he did. Somewhere along the line it had just become easier, more comfortable, less nerve-wracking to avoid guys altogether.

"I think you're nuts," Tania pronounced. "I mean, what about Denny Green or Stan Blackman? You've had guys interested in you before."

"Not the ones I wanted interested."

"Maybe that's because you chose the ones who wouldn't be."

"Self-fulfilling prophecy, Ms. Freud?" Cady glanced over from the menu on the screen.

"I just think you haven't given guys in general much of a chance. Why not try with Hurst?"

"Are you nuts? That would be like sticking a kid with a learner's permit in a demolition derby. No thanks."

"It would be interesting."

"So would skydiving without a parachute, at least for the first couple of minutes. Damon Hurst is in and out of here. And no," she said as Tania's eyes brightened, "before you start, I don't need in and out, either metaphorically or literally."

"Well, I think that you're the one who's nuts," Tania said, picking up the carton of broccoli beef. "I'd go for him in a heartbeat."

"Then why don't you?" Cady asked tartly.

"Maybe I will. Maybe I'll just…" Tania trailed off, staring at Cady. "You've got a thing for him," she said with slowly dawning delight.

"I don't have a thing for him," Cady retorted. "I told you, I don't want any part of him."

"Oh yeah, you do."

"I want him gone."

"Liar."

"Watch the movie," Cady grumbled.

Chapter Three

"No tuna at all?" Damon asked. He sat in the tiny nook off the kitchen that served as his office. Smaller than a phone booth, the space held a little counter just wide enough for a laptop and a phone, high enough that he could either sit on a tall chair or stand and look out across the kitchen.

"No more tuna, not today. We're already out," the fish vendor said over the phone.

"How about skate wing?"

"We got some nice scallops," he offered.

It was an education in what was possible, Damon told himself. "Fifteen pounds of that."

"I got you down for haddock and lobster, also. Standing order. You still want it?"

"For now. Things will be changing soon, though." He hoped to God. With a scowl, Damon ended the call.

He wasn't used to not being able to get whatever he wanted

delivered to his door, from suppliers no more than an hour or two away. Of course, he also wasn't used to getting off work at midnight to find that the entire town had rolled up the sidewalks. After hours of fast, hard, demanding work, he needed time to come down. In Manhattan, that had meant a bar or nightclub. In Grace Harbor, it appeared to mean his living room.

Then again, there was something to be said for getting enough sleep to be at work early. The kitchen, at this hour, was quiet. Only Roman was in, standing at the stainless steel counter that paralleled the row of stoves that ran along one side wall; together, the two formed the line, where the bulk of the entrées came together during lunch or dinner service. Opposite the end of the line was the little corner bay where hot and cold appetizers were put together; between the apps station and the end of the line ran a crosswise aisle that led through a doorway to the dishwashing station and the back door and the walk-in.

Which brought him back to fish.

"What kind of a fish market sells out of tuna at seven in the morning, Roman?" he asked.

Roman glanced up, but his knife never ceased moving. "A fish market that sells a lot of tuna to Japan for sushi, Chef. You could probably get some shipped in."

"I'm not going to get it shipped in when it's fished right here." He walked past Roman to the boxes of produce that had been delivered that morning. Farm Fresh From California, the labels proclaimed, but how fresh could it be if it had been shipped across the country by truck or plane or train? And why were they getting goods from California when New Jersey and Florida were probably growing everything they needed by this time of year? Doing business in Maine was proving more of a challenge than he'd expected.

At least the kitchen was in good shape, all white walls and gleaming counters and terra-cotta tiled floor. The powerful fans at the ceiling were silent at this hour. When the stoves were fired up and the unbroken surface of their tops became one giant radiator, the fans and AC would kick into gear. Not that it would help much. Once the dinner rush was on and all the cooks were working on the line, all the air-conditioning in the world wouldn't keep the temperature down.

At this hour, though, the kitchen was cool and empty, quiet save for the soft tick of Roman's knife.

Damon turned back to his tiny office, the walls lined with clipboards that held the order sheets, a separate one for each day of the week. It was an organized system and Roman had kept it up, Damon would give him that. Actually, he'd give him a whole lot more, having seen the guy work the line during service the day before. A good man with a knife, Roman, and he ran a clean station. He moved easily from the grill to sauté to apps as necessary, turning out clean, consistently plated dishes each time.

Damon had the facility, he had the staff. Now it was up to him to come up with the right food.

The Sextant's menu currently ran to entrées like baked haddock, steamed lobster, steak. Basic, satisfying fare, good enough for guests who didn't want to deal with going into Kennebunk or Portland, but nothing that was going to bring anybody to the restaurant on purpose.

The thing to do was to hold on to the New England traditions but rework them, take the lobster and blueberries and turn them into something more than the sum of the parts. It was that aspect of cooking that he really loved, letting his imagination take flight, playing with flavors, mixing elements to come up with a new twist that made the taste buds sit up and take notice.

Of course, the thing to do was to go gradually. He'd ride with the current menu for a week while he developed the new dishes and Roman and the rest of the line cooks perfected making them. Then they'd rotate a few dishes in each night until at the end of the second week they'd be serving a revamped menu featuring the familiar flavors but taken to a new level.

The restaurant currently had two stars in the guidebooks. The McBains were hoping for three; Damon had vowed to get them four. Of course, that had been before he'd found out what kind of food stocks he had to work with. A look at suppliers and food cost requirements meant jiggering things a bit, but he could still do it. He was going to blow away Ian and Amanda McBain. And their daughter.

Especially their stubborn, opinionated daughter.

She was definitely an original. Nice enough looking, he supposed, though you'd hardly know she was aware of it. He was used to women who flirted, women who were experts at polishing their own allure. He wasn't sure he could remember ever meeting a woman who just purely didn't give a damn about making a good impression, on him or anyone else. As annoying as it was, he had to give her credit. Her redhead's skin might look milky smooth but that tough, compact body could go toe-to-toe with anyone.

He remembered her scent and smiled. Going toe-to-toe with her could be kind of intriguing.

The phone rang and he picked it up absently. "Hurst."

"Seven o'clock and already at work," Paul Descour said in his lightly accented English. "I'm happy to see it."

"That makes one of us," Damon said, stifling a yawn.

"You can sleep when you're dead, my friend. You cannot build a world-class restaurant from the grave."

"Now, there's a sprightly thought to start out the day. Was that the only reason you called, to cheer me up?"

"I called to see how your new venture is going."

"Oh, great. I'm learning how to make meals without fresh produce."

"No green market?"

"I'm working on it. So far, I can mostly tell you what they don't grow within a hundred miles of here."

"So it is a challenge. It will show you what you are made of."

"It's not what I'm made of that I'm worried about," Damon said.

"You have always been resourceful. I am sure you will find a way. And how is the restaurant?"

"It's got possibilities," Damon allowed. "The kitchen setup's good. A little small for the size of the dining room but it's not a problem right now. We've got enough tables to do a hundred and fifty covers a night but we've had less than a quarter of that since I've been here."

"It is okay to start small. You are still working out the bugs."

"Bugs are definitely not on the menu."

"And that is a good thing. The health department just closed La Dolce Vida for violations," Descour said, referring to Manhattan's Italian restaurant of the moment.

Damon shook his head. "Marco never was much on taking care of the details."

"You may have had your faults, but you always kept a clean kitchen," Descour said.

"I learned from a tough boss."

"You did not learn everything from me, my friend. Some of what you know is a gift. Some of what you know I want no responsibility for," he added before Damon could be pleased. "I did not like it when you were pissing your life away."

Funny how the rebuke didn't sting the way it would have from Damon's father. Then again, Colonel Brandon Hurst would never have leavened the criticism with a compliment, or meant the compliment if he had. It would have been one more condemnation in a lifetime's worth, one more bit of proof that Damon had fallen short of expectations. Paul said it because he wanted better for Damon; the colonel would have said it because he wanted a better reflection on himself.

Which was an opportunity for its own kind of small revenge. However much Damon had squirmed at the exaggerations, rumors and outright lies the tabloids had printed about him, he'd always enjoyed imagining the colonel's reaction, coming across them in some grocery store.

He never knew for sure it had happened because he hadn't spoken to his father in nearly a decade.

If anyone had suggested to him that his drive for success stemmed from a need to prove himself to his father, Damon would have scoffed. Paul, though, Paul mattered. The problem was that Damon had no good answer for him. Mistakes, he'd probably—okay, certainly—made, but it was pointless to regret them now. The thing was to learn. If he'd done that much, then they could be filed under interesting experiences, no harm, no foul.

"What's done is done," he said. "I can't change it. I'm more interested in what happens next."

"I shall be curious to see," Descour said.

"I'm even more interested in finding a way to get produce that hasn't spent the day soaking up exhaust fumes in some cargo bay."

"I shall be curious to see how you manage that, too."

"I'll let you know when I figure it out."

After he'd ended the conversation and hung up, Damon stared at the phone before him for a moment. "Hey, Roman," he said aloud. "What do you know about foraging?"

Early morning was Cady's favorite time. The day felt fresh and new, the air so crisp, even in May, that her breath showed as she loaded bags of Compass Rose yard waste into the bed of her battered pickup. The guests were all asleep, the employees yet to show up. She had the grounds to herself, just her and Grace Harbor, the quiet lap of the water against the rocks punctuated by the cries of the gulls.

Some people took time to find their place in the world. Cady had always known she belonged in Maine. Her brother, Walker, might have moved to Manhattan; her sister, Max, might have tried out Chicago before coming back to settle in Portland. As far as Cady was concerned, there was nowhere else she'd rather be than on this particular bit of coast. Life down east might not always be easy, but it satisfied her soul.

Of course, these days she had a bit more than her soul to worry about. After six years of working for another landscaper in the area, she'd decided to hang out her own shingle two years before. Be her own boss, her thinking went, though she hadn't quite realized at the time that being her own boss really meant that *everyone* was her boss, particularly her clients. To date, the best thing she could say was that she was keeping her head above water.

Barely.

One challenge was that the population of Grace Harbor was a whopping five thousand people, though that quadrupled when the summer tourists descended in droves. Another was that the Maine growing season was so short. Hard to make a living growing things when those things only grew from May to September.

But that was the job she'd taken on, so from May to September, she worked, she cultivated, she pasted a smile on her face and made nice until her jaws hurt. And in the winter, she put a plow blade on her truck and prayed for snow.

Still, she was making progress. Her old truck would have to last a few more years but the new greenhouse gave her a critical advantage in growing her own stock that would pay off big down the line. She'd acquired a few steady clients— businesses, rental property owners, her uncle Lenny at the marina. She'd scrape along, even if the Compass Rose was still her biggest account.

Cady settled another bag in the bed of her truck and turned

back to the pile. It didn't matter that the inn was family owned, her parents had always treated it as a business, insisting on paying her just as they would any other groundskeeper. And because Cady was in business, too, she'd felt honor bound to negotiate long and hard with them over the terms. She still considered it something of a coup that she'd fast-talked her father so that he didn't realize he'd signed a contract that paid her less than he had his last groundskeeper.

It was her business, and she'd do what she wanted, including offer a family discount, even if the family didn't know. It wasn't as if she was going to go broke.

Yet.

She wasn't so sure about her parents, though. The past couple of years had been increasingly tight, even as repairs on the nearly hundred-year-old main building mounted up. They definitely needed to make a move to bring in more traffic.

Hiring an unstable guy like Damon Hurst wasn't making a move, though. It was desperation.

Damon Hurst. Just the thought of his name had her fuming, and if that didn't, the memory of his easy smirk did. Cady knew about him. Oh, she knew all about him whether she wanted to or not, courtesy of Tania, who was a complete junkie for his show.

"I don't care about cooking, Tania," she'd pleaded at one of their weekly get-togethers. "Can't we just watch a movie?"

"It's almost over. Besides, how hard is it? Don't you want to look at that face?" Tania had returned, eyes gleaming. "Don't you want to see how long it takes him to yell at one of his chefs during the competition?"

"No. I want to see vampires and car chases and preferably something blowing up. I don't want to see Damon Hurst."

Well, she'd have to see him now, Cady thought, at least for the two or three weeks he'd probably stick around. She thumped another bag of yard waste into her truck. How he'd managed to con her parents into trusting him was anybody's guess. Why, was even more perplexing. He had to have options in the city, job offers that paid a whole lot better than her parents could afford. Why come all the way up to a little dot-on-the-map Maine town? Could he really be that hard up? And if he was, did they really want him?

It was a fiasco waiting to happen. The guy hadn't even bothered to come look at the restaurant and meet the people he was going to work with before taking the job. That wasn't the behavior of a man who gave a hoot about his staff—or his performance. No way was he planning on being there for the long haul.

Gritting her teeth, she slammed another bag down.

"You're going to split one of those open if you don't watch it," a voice said behind her, making her jump.

She knew before she turned it was him.

He wore jeans and the same bomber jacket he'd had on the day she'd met him, his dark hair loose and pushed back behind his ears. He still hadn't bothered to shave; even in sunlight, his eyes looked only two or three shades away from black. Not that she was noticing. Good-looking guys didn't get to her, Cady reminded herself.

She spared him another glance. "Well, you're up and around early."

He smiled faintly. "Not a lot of nightlife around here."

"Life in Grace Harbor. Sorry to disappoint you."

"I didn't say I was disappointed."

She bent back to her rubbish pile. "I'm so relieved."

This time he laughed outright. "Nice to see you're in good form again today."

"I'm in good form every day," she said, tossing an armload of rhododendron branches into the bed. "Get used to it."

He looked her up and down. "I'm not even going to touch that one."

She flushed and grabbed another load of branches from the previous day's pruning to toss into the bed. "So what brings you out here so early?"

"Maybe I just wanted some fresh air."

"It's all around you. Knock yourself out." She turned to find him already handing her the next bag from her pile. She hesitated, then took the brown paper sack from him. "Thanks."

"Don't mention it. What's McBain Landscaping?" He nodded at the magnetic sign on her truck door. "I thought it was Compass Rose."

"The Compass Rose is my parents'. I've got my own business."

"Planting stuff?"

She scowled. "Yeah, I plant stuff, you fry stuff."

"Okay." Brown paper crackled as he handed her a bag of leaves. "Let's start again. Along the lines of frying stuff, Roman says you're the person to talk to about the farmers' market."

"You've met him, finally. Good for you."

He gave her a narrow-eyed look. "The farmers' market?"

"What do you want to know? Directions?"

"Among other things."

"Kennebunk has a market but it doesn't open until June. This time of year you'll have to go to Portland."

"How long's the drive?"

"As long as an hour, depending on traffic." At his whistle, Cady shrugged. "It's in town. It's tricky to find parking. If you're smart, you'll do like Nathan did. Skip the market and have what you want trucked in from suppliers." Before she'd even gotten the words out, Damon was already shaking his head.

"No trucks. I want local. Fresh."

"People in hell. Ice water," she countered. "It's too early in the season here to have much of anything to harvest unless it's greenhouse grown."

He picked up an armload of lilac branches and tossed them over the side of the truck into the bed. "Roman says Nathan supplemented shipments with veg he bought locally."

"When he could." Cady added an armload of her own.

"Roman says he's been going with local stuff, too. Actually—" Damon flicked an assessing glance at her "—he said you were the one who went to the market for him. Said he'd never have made it through if it hadn't been for you."

Cady shifted uncomfortably. "Roman talks too much."

"Not necessarily."

"Don't get any ideas. He was shorthanded and working his butt off, so I pitched in to help. It's not an ongoing program. I've got a business to run." She shut the tailgate of the truck. "You want the farmers' market, big guy, that's your job. I'd be happy to write down directions for you."

"Better yet, go with me."

"Hello? Business to run?" She tapped the side of the truck.

"Just this once, that's all. Show me around, introduce me to the people you do business with."

"Money's the best introducer there is."

"And you know as well as I do that business is about relationships." He gave her a second glance. "Then again, maybe you haven't figured that out."

"I've got all the relationships I need."

"You might be surprised. The right one could change your whole world view."

"My world view is fine, thanks very much."

"Look, just give me tomorrow morning," he said in exasperation. "I'll keep it quick."

She reached in her pocket for her keys. "Tomorrow won't work. They only hold the market twice a week—today and Saturdays."

"Twice a week? For a town with as many restaurants as Portland? You're kidding."

"It's May. It's Maine. You're lucky the market's even open this time of year."

"Don't sound so happy about it."

She'd promised to be civil, Cady reminded herself, and even for her, she wasn't doing a very good job. She let out a long, slow breath. "All right. It just so happens that I'm working a job today for a summer client, so they won't know if I push them off until later. If you're obsessed about having me take you to the market, I'll take you. One hour only," she warned. "And you'd better be ready to go now. I've got a job site to be at this afternoon." She opened her driver's door.

Damon glanced at the rubbish-filled truck bed. "Are you going to take it like that?"

"What, you think people are going to steal my dead leaves?"

"No, because I figure it's all going to blow out by the time we hit the highway. Let me drive."

"I didn't know Manhattanites knew how to."

"I've seen it on TV," he said.

"Forget it. I know where we're going. For your information, the dump's on the way. I was already planning to stop."

He eyed her. "You just want to be behind the wheel."

"That's right," she said, getting in. "Nobody moves me from the driver's seat."

His slow smile set something fluttering in her stomach. "We'll see about that."

Chapter Four

It was what she got for being nice, Cady thought as they drove up the highway to Portland. If she'd thought twice, she'd never have agreed to be stuck in the tight confines of a vehicle with Damon Hurst. He sprawled comfortably in the passenger seat, his lanky frame making the cab seem very small. It was impossible to ignore him. However much she tried to pay attention to the road, he was what she noticed.

He didn't bother to make conversation. She wasn't sure if that was a relief or if it left her to focus all the more on him. He just sat there in his leather jacket and stubbled chin, looking like something out of a blue jeans ad, looking like—

Cady cursed and stomped on the brakes as the car ahead slowed suddenly.

"A decent following distance might help with that," Damon said mildly, though she noticed he reached up to grab the overhead handhold.

"If you're going to be a backseat driver, change seats."

"You don't have a backseat."

"I know. So relax and enjoy the scenery." She whipped over into another lane and onto the exit ramp.

"I can't see it with my eyes closed," he said through his teeth as the truck swayed with the quick succession of turns she made on the city streets.

Cady caught sight of a parking space and punched it to get through a yellow light and to the opening. "Well, you can open your eyes up now, sweet pea. We're there."

"Thank God," Damon said and slowly, carefully, released his grip. "Next time, I'm driving."

"There won't be a next time."

"I'm still driving."

The square before them was filled with the color and hubbub of the farmers' market. Canvas-tented booths in blue and green and yellow displayed boxes of lettuce in a bewildering variety, pyramids of the fall's apples and potatoes and cabbage. Hothouse tomatoes provided flashes of red next to the vivid purple and green of rhubarb. Even though it was barely eight, the market was bustling.

Catching sight of a stand selling pastries, Cady made a quick beeline for it.

Damon came to a stop beside her. "What are you doing?"

"Breakfast," she told him. "It's the least I deserve after making the drive."

"Are you kidding? I'm the one who ought to be rewarded for surviving."

"Fine. You can buy us both drinks. I'll take a Coke."

"At eight in the morning?"

"It's the best one of the day. What do you want here?" She gestured at the pastry and pulled out her wallet.

"A corn muffin, I guess," Damon said, lining up before the coffee urn.

"A corn muffin and a cheese Danish," Cady ordered.

They made their way over to a bench, exchanging booty. He watched her as she took a bite of Danish, washing it down with a swig of cola.

"You know you'll die young eating like that?"

"That's what people tell me," she said, licking crumbs off her fingers with relish.

"Cream cheese and Coke. I don't even want to think about what that combination tastes like." He took a swallow of coffee.

"It's not about the taste, it's about the sugar rush, although you'd be surprised if you tried it."

He gave her a pained look. "Someone needs to educate your palate."

"My palate's doing just fine, thank you very much. Okay—" she balled up her napkin "—let's get going."

Damon swallowed the last of his muffin. "That didn't count as part of the hour, by the way." He tossed his trash into the nearby barrel. "The clock starts now."

"Then get going."

It wasn't what she'd expected. She'd thought it would be like going grocery shopping—pick and buy, pick and buy. Instead, Damon wandered down the rows aimlessly, stopping at this stand to sniff at a shiny red apple, that one to weigh a bunch of rhubarb in his hands and stare thoughtfully into space.

"You know, that's the fourth place you've checked out the lettuce," she said as he examined yet another head of brushy green stuff.

"Do you buy a car at the first place you go?" he asked, then shook his head. "Never mind, I've seen your truck."

Cady scowled. "What's wrong with my truck? It got you here, didn't it?"

He put down the head of lettuce and walked to the next stand. "Thank God for small favors."

"It's under no obligation to get you home, you know. Speaking of home, when, exactly, are you going to start buying things? You are going to eventually, aren't you?"

"Maybe. I don't know." He stopped at a vendor selling mushrooms and picked up a deformed orange thing that looked as though it had grown under someone's back steps. Cady repressed a shudder. Her notion of cuisine ran toward pizzas and burgers, not something nasty that looked like an alien life form.

"If you're not going to buy anything then what, exactly, are we doing here?"

"Recon." He gave her an amused glance. "I want to see what's out there, what I can get around here. If I can find something for tonight's special, so much the better. Like these." He picked up a different mushroom.

"What are they?" She stared suspiciously at the pointy, honeycombed fungus.

"Morels. Unbelievable flavor and texture."

She watched as he sifted through the pile, hands quick, picking some mushrooms for his bag, leaving others. "I'll take your word for it."

"What I need now are some ramps," he said after he'd finished with the cashier. "I'll sauté them up in a little ragout and put it over a poached haddock."

"I'm sure they'll all come running. What are ramps, anyway?"

"Wild baby leeks that grow in the woods this time of year. They taste like a cross between onions and garlic. I can't believe nobody's got any here. We'll have to hunt some down." He started walking again.

She trailed along after him. "Not we, you. I've got a job, remember?"

"How about you quit and come be my forager? You grow stuff, you'd be good at it."

"I brought you to the market. Wasn't that enough?"

"It would be if it was a real market." He shook his head. "This is pathetic. Most of it's from last year."

The criticism had her raising her chin. "I told you, it's too early for fresh produce here. It won't really get going until July."

"The green market in Manhattan had ramps and asparagus and squash blossoms last week."

"And it's four temperature zones away from us," she defended. "This is Maine. We have snow until April. We grow what we can. If you want more of a choice, feel free to drive down to Boston. In fact, feel free to keep going."

He studied her. "You don't want me here, do you?"

Cady opened her mouth, closed it. "It's not a matter of what I want. It's my parents' business and they think you're the right guy for the job."

"You're evading the question."

"Okay, how about this? I've seen the headlines. I know your style. You don't fit here."

He smiled. "You don't believe in soft-pedaling things, do you?"

"Why waste the time?"

"And you think you know all about me."

"Given all the press you've generated, it's kind of hard not to."

"Now who's wasting time?" he countered. "Half of those stories are exaggerations, the other half are outright lies."

She folded her arms. "So, what, you didn't throw people out of your restaurant?"

"Okay, I might have asked one or two people to leave early on," he admitted. "You've got a restaurant, you know how they can be. In fact, I'd be a little shocked if you've never thrown someone out yourself."

"The customer is always right," she reminded him, not bothering to add that she'd never had the choice.

"That's funny coming from someone whose operating assumption seems to be that everyone else in the world is wrong but them."

Her cheeks tinted. "We're not talking about me."

"I am."

"Stop changing the subject. This is about you. Maybe I didn't see you punch your sous chef but I know you yelled at him because I saw it."

"You saw it?"

She could have bitten her tongue. "My girlfriend was watching *Chef's Challenge*."

"You don't say."

"And I know the story of the woman in your office is true because the husband named you in the divorce proceedings."

"Well, well. You have been studying up," he said and something flickered in the depths of his eyes.

"What, are you trying to say it didn't happen?" she challenged.

"I think that's between her and me." He reached out to catch the hood strings of the jacket she wore. "The same way it would be between you and me if anything happened."

"Nothing's going to happen with us," Cady returned, but suddenly it was hard to catch a breath.

"Mmm, careful what you say," Damon murmured, tugging her forward a bit. "That sounds like a dare."

She should have been smacking his hand away. She should have been turning on her heel to go. She couldn't understand why all she was doing was looking into those eyes as he leaned closer and wondering what it would be like if—

"Hey, Cady!" A shout came from behind her, releasing her from the spell.

She did move to smack Damon's hand away then, but he'd already released her. She turned away without another word, not trusting herself.

"Pete," she called and crossed over to the booth where a burly man with a graying close-trimmed beard waved at her.

"Hey, good to see you. Howya doing?" he asked from behind a table covered with baskets of tomatoes.

"Good. How's Jenny?" she asked, thinking of his neat, compact wife.

"Good, thanks."

Damon walked up to the stand to look at the tomatoes gleaming ruby red in the sun.

"Nice." He picked one up, nodding to Pete. "Hothouse?"

"Yep." Pete adjusted the NAPA cap on his grizzled hair. "Early Girl beefsteaks."

Damon sniffed the tomato he held and put it down in favor of another, turning it over in his hands. "How many greenhouses?" he asked.

"Two. Careful how you handle that."

"What's the square footage?"

Pete's eyes narrowed suspiciously. "You lookin' to buy my tomatoes or my greenhouse?"

"Pete." Cady stepped forward. "I want you to meet our new chef at the Sextant, Damon Hurst. Damon, meet Pete Tebeau."

"The new chef? Why didn't you say so? Pleased to meetcha." Damon found his hand enveloped by a hand the approximate size of an oven mitt. "Does that mean we're not going to see you here anymore, Cady?"

"If I've got anything to say about it. Not that seeing you isn't the highlight of my day, Pete." She grinned at the guy and suddenly she looked young, mischievous and downright pretty.

And Damon kept his jaw from dropping, only just. She was flirting with the guy. This scratchy-tongued woman who had turned being a curmudgeon into a holy calling was joking around, chatting up a guy old enough to be her father.

"The highlight of your day? You'd be amazed at how many women tell me that." Pete didn't miss a beat.

Cady snorted. "You better hope Jenny doesn't get wind of it."

"She's the one who says it most of all."

It had all the hallmarks of an old game between them. It had all the signs of a long friendship. And he couldn't stop watching her.

"So, how are the plans for the big weekend?" Cady asked.

Pete's eyes gleamed. "Great, thanks to you. We're in one of your cabins, harbor view, they said."

"I'll make sure Lynne puts you in guesthouse two," Cady said. "It's got the prettiest view of the water. You can sit out on the deck in the morning with your coffee. Jenny's going to love it."

"I hope so. I want her to be happy."

"After twenty-five years, Pete, I think you can be pretty sure she's happy."

"Yeah, but she's had a rough time lately, what with losing her dad and all." He took his cap off and turned it around in his hands. "I want to give her a special anniversary, something she'll remember."

Like a weekend at the Compass Rose, Damon translated. "You're coming to the inn for your anniversary?" he asked.

Tebeau nodded. "This weekend. Usually I just take her out and buy her a lobster. I figured twenty-five years deserved something more, though. This young lady helped."

The young lady in question flushed and looked away.

"Tell you what," Damon said. "Come to the restaurant for dinner while you're there. I'll make you a special meal. Off the menu, I mean, just for you two. What does your wife like to eat?"

Tebeau thought a moment. "Garlic, shrimp, crab cakes. And mushrooms," he added.

Sometimes you just had to go with your instincts. Damon picked up two baskets of tomatoes. "I know just what to make for her. You know anyone who sells ramps here?"

"Ramps?" Tebeau took the tomatoes and set them on the scale.

"Wild leeks. White flowers, green leaves about so big." He measured. "I sauté them up with morels and asparagus and you'll think you've died and gone to heaven. If I can find them. Got any ideas?"

"Maybe." Pete took the money Damon offered. "Old Gus Cattrall next door to me, he's got all kinda stuff growing in the woods over on his place."

"Great," Damon said. "Does he have a stall here?"

Tebeau shook his head. "Naw. Mostly he just sells stuff out of a cart on the road. Never seen him put out—what did you call them, ramps? But if he's got 'em growing, I bet he'd be happy to let you pick them yourself."

"Just tell me who to call or where to go."

Pete handed Damon his change and loaded the tomatoes into a box. "Thing is, Gus isn't likely to cotton to strangers walking around his property. He knows you, though, Cady. You'd better come instead."

"Me?" she asked blankly. "But—"

"Sure. This guy's got my curiosity up. Why don't you come over to my place tomorrow morning about six? We can catch Gus before he gets working. If he's got any of those ramps growing you can bet he'll know where and we can just pick 'em. Easy as pie."

"Easy as pie," Cady said under her breath. "All right, Pete, sure. As long as you've got time."

"Absolutely."

"Then I'll see you tomorrow. Damon—" she directed him a thunderous look "—we'd better get going."

He had better sense than to argue. Cady marched to the end of the row in silence, though he could see from the set of her shoulders that she had plenty to say. He figured he'd just wait her out.

He didn't have to wait long.

"Happy with yourself?" she demanded as soon as they were out of the square.

Now was not the time to smile, he reminded himself as he followed her down the street. "Happy why?"

"Oh, you got your trip to the market, now you're going to get your wild onions."

"Leeks."

"Whatever." She stopped beside her truck. "You're good at getting people to do what you want, aren't you? You're a regular puppeteer."

He couldn't help laughing at that as he set the tomatoes and mushrooms in the truck bed. "I'm flattered that you think so much of me."

She glowered. "Oh, I think of you, all right. I think all kinds of things about you."

"Good." In the sunlight, her hair gleamed cinnamon and copper. He could see a light dusting of freckles on the bridge of her nose. "You know," he said as she opened her mouth to continue, "for someone who tries to come off so tough, that was a pretty nice thing you did for Pete."

She stared at him, momentarily disarmed. "He's a friend," she muttered finally. "I want them to have a nice time."

"They will, thanks to you."

"And you," she said, then blinked as though the thought had ambushed her.

"Correct me if I'm wrong, but I believe you just said something nice to me."

The flush that spread across her cheeks made her look even more delectable. "Don't try to distract me."

There was something that kind of delighted him about that bemused look she got on her face when she felt she was losing control of the situation. "Oh, I don't know, I'm beginning to think distracting you could be interesting. Very interesting," he added.

He reached out, then, to touch, running a finger across her cheek to her chin. Softer than he'd expected. She might dress and act like a tomboy but Cady McBain was all girl. Her eyes flashed with surprise, awareness, the hazel green darkening to amber. He saw the desire flicker even as he felt it himself.

All it would take was bridging that distance to find out how it would be with her. He couldn't help wondering. And even as he told himself it wasn't smart, he leaned in toward her.

The chirp of a horn had them both jolting apart.

Damon snapped his head around to see a blue Escort packed with a trio of what looked like college-age girls.

"Hey, you leaving?" the gum-chewing passenger called out the window.

"Definitely," Cady answered from behind him, opening the driver's door.

He turned to her. "Why the rush?" he asked.

"We've done everything we need to do here."

"You think so?"

"I know so," she said. "We're done with this."

"No." Damon got in on the other side and shut the door. "That's one thing I'm pretty sure of. We're not done with this by a long shot."

Chapter Five

She couldn't believe she'd let it happen. Cady pulled her truck to a stop in the employee side of the parking lot the next morning and stared at the box of ramps next to her. Bad enough that he'd manipulated her into grubbing around some forest glen looking for his wild leeks, but he'd *gotten* to her. One minute she'd been ready to put him in his place, which was as far from her as she could manage. The next, she was gaping at him as if she was hypnotized, as if she didn't have a brain in her head.

He'd charmed her. Her, the one who prided herself on keeping it together, on being immune to good-looking guys. The one who was never again going to make herself vulnerable to some guy who thought the world should be at his feet.

And the worst part was that he hadn't even had to try. All he'd had to do was to make nice to her in that voice that sent those little bubbles fizzing through her veins, look at her with those eyes and touch her.

And touch her.

Involuntarily, Cady shivered. It didn't mean anything. It had been so long since anybody had touched her outside of family, that was all. That was why it had affected her. It wasn't him, certainly not him.

Definitely not.

That didn't mean she wouldn't be smart to keep her distance. While she sincerely doubted that Damon Hurst had any real interest in her, she had no plans to give him any opportunities. She checked her watch and got out of the truck with the box of greens. Best to drop off the ramps and get to work.

Her steps faltered a bit when she discovered the back door to the kitchen unlocked and the lights on. For an instant, she debated just leaving the box outside the back door. She hadn't spent a backbreaking hour picking them only to see someone walk all over them by accident, though. Besides, she was many things but she wasn't a wimp. She'd go inside just as she'd planned.

It was probably only Roman there, anyway. It wasn't like Mr. Celebrity Chef was going to be up at the crack of dawn doing prep. And even if it were him, it wasn't a problem, she told herself quickly. She'd been caught off guard at the market, that was all. This time, she was prepared for any games he might play. Everything would be fine.

And if she held her breath when she walked through the passageway into the kitchen and put the box on one of the stainless steel counters, it was nobody's business but her own. She'd fulfilled her obligation. All she had to do was—

"Stop." Damon's voice sounded in her ear. Adrenaline flooded through her. Every muscle in her body tensed. She moved to turn.

"No. Close your eyes," he ordered.

Cady bristled. "Who do you think—"

"Just do it."

And she found herself obeying, as much out of surprise as anything. Her heart thudded in her chest. He was right in front of her; she could feel him, sense the heat from his body.

Feel his breath feathering across her face.

"Open your mouth."

Pulse jittery, she did.

"Tell me what you think of this," he murmured. His fingers were hard and warm against her lips and cheek. The contact sent shock rippling through her, all of her nerve endings coming to the alert. Then she stilled because he slipped a tidbit of something that smelled incredible into her mouth.

And tasted even better.

She bit down and exquisite flavor burst through her mouth. Crisp, soft, rich, savory, it was a glorious blend of taste and texture that bombarded all of her senses, occupied every taste bud. She wanted to savor, she wanted to swallow. She wanted more. She couldn't prevent a humming moan of pleasure.

"I take it that means you approve?"

The words dragged her back to the moment. Her eyes flew open to see Damon standing there, staring at her, intent. Something skittered around in her stomach. He watched her unwaveringly, but he didn't watch her with the gaze of a chef interested in his creations.

He watched her with the eyes of a man who'd just pleasured a woman, not with taste but with touch.

The breath backed up in her lungs. He was close, way too close in his checked trousers and whites, the apron tied around his lean hips. She swore she felt the air heat around them.

It was just the line of stoves across the room, that was all, Cady told herself unsteadily. The place was always hot. That was why he had his sleeves rolled up. Her bad luck that years of demanding kitchen work had left him with the kind of powerful, sinewy forearms that made her more aware than ever of the strength and purpose driving that rangy body.

"Was it good?" he asked.

"Good?" she echoed blankly.

"The food. Did you like it?"

"Oh." By sheer force of will she dragged herself out of the sensory overload and stepped away for her own sanity. "Good, yeah, good doesn't begin to cover it. What was that?"

"Judging by the way you looked just now, something that belongs on the menu. It's an appetizer," he elaborated. "A *croustillant*. Squab, fois gras, morel emulsion in brek dough."

"You're talking to someone who eats pizza and macaroni and cheese. Translate."

"Ah. Pigeon, duck liver and mushroom sauce in pastry."

Her brow creased. "I think I liked it better when I didn't know."

"Sorry, I'm fresh out of cheese Danish."

"Too bad. I'm not much for fancy food."

"Oh yeah?" He leaned against the counter. "For not being much for fancy food, you seemed pretty into it. Maybe you should spend less time worrying about what you don't want to like and just go ahead and like it."

She had the uncomfortable feeling he was talking about more than food. She raised her chin. "Thanks for the sage advice, Yoda. I'll keep it in mind. Here are your ramps, by the way. At least Gus thinks they're ramps. If not, you've got a bunch of matching weeds."

"They look right to me," Damon said, picking one up to inspect it.

"Great. I hope they rock your world. I'm out of here." She headed for the door before she could start staring at his forearms again.

"Wait."

"I've got to go."

"Just hang on a minute, will you?" He followed her.

"I already got up at the crack of dawn for you. What do

you want now?" she asked, a tiny thread of desperation in her voice. She turned with her hand on the latch, heart hammering, to find him behind her.

"I wanted to say thanks," he said softly. "You didn't have to do this. It wasn't your job and you still took the time."

She shifted uncomfortably. "I did it for Pete and his wife."

"I like that all the more." He took another step closer.

Her pulse thundered in her ears. "I should get to work." She moistened her lips. "You should get back to work."

He looked down at her as though she was the next course on the menu. "We should do a lot of things."

"We shouldn't do this."

"You don't know, you might like it."

Something stirred again in her stomach. It was a risk she couldn't take. "It doesn't matter," she reminded herself as much as him. "I know what I don't like to like and I stick with it."

And with a turn and a step, she was out the back door.

It was a good thing, Damon told himself as he stood staring through the screen at Cady's retreating back. He had no business kissing her, however much he'd had the urge.

And he'd been having the urge a lot in the past few days.

It made no sense. She certainly wasn't like the women he usually went after. He already knew what she thought of him. Anyway, he didn't need to be distracted just then by a woman, especially a permanently cranky woman who'd made it her mission to irritate him. However much it might fascinate him to see her hard shell dissolve, to watch her gaze blur and her mouth soften, she wasn't for him.

But still he stood watching as she walked away.

Maybe if he hadn't seen that look on her face, the complete and utter absorption in pleasure when she'd tasted the *croustillant*. He'd expected her to like it. He'd never in a million years expected the reaction he'd gotten. He'd watched her face and all he could think was that this was how she'd look at climax. And he'd felt himself tighten as though he'd just brought her there.

And he was doing himself absolutely no good by thinking about it. He was working for her parents, Damon reminded himself, walking back into the kitchen. He was supposed to be changing his life, not just taking his act from Manhattan to Maine. Cady was right; they had no business doing anything about whatever it was that was suddenly simmering between them.

But as a chef he knew that the longer you left something on simmer, the stronger it became.

There was a brisk ticking noise from the kitchen. Roman, he saw, on the clock and jumping straight into work.

"You're in early," Damon said as the sous chef began to deftly and precisely cube the carrots that they'd use to make the stock for the lobster bisque.

Roman shrugged. "It's gotten to be a habit."

"It's a good way to get ahead." Damon reached for his knives. "How long have you been cooking, Roman?"

"Going on three years. Took a job cooking the summer after I got out of college. It stuck."

"College, huh? What was your degree in?"

"Business. Kitchen's for me, though." He flashed a smile. "My mom about had a stroke. All that tuition money down the drain."

"Not necessarily." Damon started cleaning beef tenderloins, the sound of his knife against the cutting board providing a brisk counterpoint to the steady tick of Roman's. "The business degree could come in handy if you ever decide to open your own place."

"No ifs about it, Chef. My wife's from Rochester. We're going to go back there in a few years and start a little place of our own. In the meantime, I'll save money, get better in the kitchen. I figure I can learn something from you. I hear you're supposed to be a pretty good cook." He glanced up, humor in his eyes.

Damon looked at the pile of perfect carrot cubes. "You look like a pretty good cook yourself. Now you've just got to work on coming up with your own food."

"I try things at home, sometimes."

"Not here?" Damon methodically sectioned the tender-loins into tournedos.

"Nathan liked to keep pretty tight control of his menu. Since he's been gone, I've pretty much just been keeping up. Not a lot of time for specials."

"Now there is. It's a good time of year for squash blossoms. Any growers sell them around here?"

Roman snorted. "Not until July. This is Maine."

"So I'm told," Damon murmured.

"You want to get them now, you'll have to have them shipped in."

Damon shook his head. "They're too delicate. Besides, you can always taste when something's been shipped."

"Skip the squash blossoms and try fiddleheads," Roman suggested. "That's one thing you can get local. They usually have them at the market."

"I must have missed them." Too busy getting distracted by Cady McBain, he thought, annoyed at himself. "I'll look again on Saturday. In the meantime, we've got ourselves some ramps. Any ideas?"

Roman considered. "Twist a few of those babies around shrimp and give 'em a nice sauté. Forget about the restaurant. You and me, we could have ourselves a nice dinner." He switched to celery, his knife a blur.

"Ramp-wrapped shrimp. You ever made it?"

"A couple of years ago when I was working down in Jersey. I put it with a cilantro-lemon sauce but it was too light to stand up to the ramps. I'd probably do it again with something stronger, maybe roasted chilis or smoked paprika."

"Try it," Damon suggested.

The knife stopped. "What, now?"

"Sure. One of the farmers from the market is coming to dinner this Saturday with his wife. They've got an anniversary to celebrate. Chef's tasting. His wife likes shrimp and garlic, by the way."

It was both opportunity and test. He watched Roman prep, first the shrimp, then the ramps. The young sous chef ran into trouble when he started to wind the green stalks around the shrimp, though.

"You need to soften them a little." Damon spoke up. "Sauté the ramps separately and then twist them around the shrimp. Or blanch them."

"A sauté would give more flavor."

"My thought, exactly."

This time, Roman worked two sauté pans, one with ramps, one with the shrimp, dusting them with spices and seasoning. He picked the hot ramps out of the pan, wrapping them around the even hotter shrimp. Tough hands, Damon thought, always a good attribute in a chef.

And an ability to multitask. Even as the wrapped shrimp were in the pan for their final sizzle, Roman pulled out a plate and prepped it with a bed of salad. He set the finished shrimp on the lettuce, drizzling them with chili sauce.

"Looks good but let me show you something." Damon picked up the shrimp pan and pulled out a second plate, this one flat and square. He didn't bother with the salad, just drizzled a small circle of the transparent red chili pan sauce in the center of the plate and then positioned three shrimp on it with their tails together and pointing in the air like inverted commas. Using a spoon, he carefully dripped small dots of bright green cilantro oil around the plate, the colors vivid against the white porcelain.

"Keep it simple," he said as he worked. "Go for height, contrast. The sauce goes on the plate, not the food. You get more visual impact that way."

"Yes, Chef." Roman admired the shrimp. "That plate looks like something else."

"Looks are good, taste is better." Damon reached out for a shrimp and swabbed it through the colored dots. He took one bite, considered. Squeezed on some lemon and took another. And another. "It's good," he said to Roman. "Add some lemon juice to the chili sauce, brighten it up. Plate it the way I showed you, finish it with some micro cilantro."

"We don't have any."

"How about the green market?"

"Not that I know of. You'll have to get it—"

"If you say shipped in, you're fired."

"Yes, Chef," Roman said.

"All right, forget about the microgreens. I'll figure something out."

He turned back to his tenderloin tournedos, sealing them in plastic storage trays, then pulled Roman's cutting board toward him. The sous chef stared, knife in hand.

"Well, get to work," Damon told him. "I'll finish this. You've got another hour to refine the sauce and write it all down and come up with a name."

"A name?"

"Sure. It's got to have a name if it's going to be our appetizer special."

Roman grinned. "Yes, Chef."

Cady always felt calmer in her greenhouse. It wasn't big as hothouses went, maybe twice the size of her living room, but it was her territory. There was a serenity in the ranks of greenery and the warm, humid air. Out here, shut away from the rest of the inn, she could put her hands in the earth and forget all about difficult guests, pesky clients, unreliable suppliers and other annoyances.

Like Damon Hurst.

She shook her head. She wasn't going there. She was not going to think about that moment in the kitchen when he'd leaned in close, when she'd seen in his eyes that he was going to kiss her. She wasn't going to wonder what it would have been like. She wasn't going to wonder how it would have felt. Nope, not going there.

You don't know, you might like it.

That was precisely the problem. She might, and that would spell disaster. A guy like Damon Hurst wasn't interested in someone like her. She'd seen him on the magazine covers wrapped cozily together with this model, that actress, and one thing Cady could say for sure was that she was not his type. Maybe he was bored, maybe she was a challenge, maybe seduction was a knee-jerk reaction for him. Whatever it was, she'd been down this road before. She wasn't about to be played.

The problem was, when he got to looking at her and talking to her, she forgot all about that. All she could do was watch his mouth and wonder.

"Don't be an idiot," she muttered and began transplanting petunia seedlings into the hanging basket that sat on the workbench before her. This was what she needed to be focusing on. She needed to be thinking about how she was going to design the perennial beds she'd spent the morning clearing out over at the Chasan place. She didn't need to be thinking about Damon Hurst.

Feet crunched on the gravel walk outside and, as though she'd conjured him by thinking, Damon opened the door across the room from her.

And serenity flew out the window.

"I thought I might find you out here," he said, stepping inside. "Hiding out?"

"Working," she said.

"Lot of that going around."

Calm had disappeared. Sanctuary was no more. She was uneasy, more than a little tongue-tied and, dammit, had butterflies. It didn't matter that she was on the other side of the room from him. Suddenly, the greenhouse seemed very small.

Damon strolled around, still in his checks and chef's whites. He should have looked ludicrously out of place and awkward. Instead, he seemed right at home. She was the one who was tense.

He turned to her. "Nice place."

Cady tried to see it through his eyes: the four long wooden tables covered with flats of pansies and snapdragons or trays of potted marigolds, the hanging baskets of geraniums and petunias, still waiting for their first blossoms. On the far side stood her workbench and the tables with pots of evening primrose, forsythia, bleeding heart. The air smelled rich and green and fertile.

"What's all this stuff?" he asked, fingering the velvety green leaf of a petunia.

"The flats are annuals—pansies, marigolds, snapdragons. The plant you're about to take a leaf off of is a petunia," she added. "It's cheaper to grow them than to buy them."

He nodded and began to wander again. Having him in her territory felt strangely intimate. The walls were opaque, the door closed, the only sound the occasional drip of water. For the first time, they were truly alone. There were no distractions, just the two of them amid the green.

"These go in the ground now?" he asked, watching her as she went back to transplanting the petunias.

"I'm starting to set some of them out in the yards I'm working on. I probably shouldn't before Mother's Day—you never know if you're going to get a frost up here—but I'm taking my chances."

"Cady McBain, extreme gardener."

"I like to live life on the edge."

"Really?" He studied her. "That's good to know."

Her skin warmed. "That wasn't an invitation."

"Do I look like I need one?"

No, he looked like the kind of guy who just went after what he wanted, she thought uneasily. She just couldn't figure out why it happened to be her.

"If you plant all this, you'll have a lot of space afterward. You could probably find a corner for a commissioned job, couldn't you?"

And there was the answer. Her eyes narrowed. "If this is about growing ramps for you, no. My hands still smell."

"Not ramps, microgreens."

"If they grow in the forest, I'm not interested."

"They don't grow in the forest."

"I'm still not interested."

He tapped his knuckles on one of the wooden tables. "They don't take much room," he offered. "Just a little dirt and water and a week or two of growing time."

"Two weeks? You know what you're going to get from two weeks of growth? Grass. Micrograss."

"Strongly flavored micrograss. They taste phenomenal, trust me. Makes all the difference in a dish."

"Then I suggest you tap into your underground chef network and find out where you can get some. In case you haven't noticed, this greenhouse is full, and when I've planted the annuals I'll be filling it up with perennials."

"The microgreens don't take a lot of space. And I need them," he said simply. "The restaurant needs them."

The thing she couldn't say no to. "What, nobody in the entire country sells them?"

"The closest supplier I could find is a guy out in the Midwest."

"And let me guess, you want local."

"Bingo," he said. "A lot of other chefs do, too. You know, this wouldn't just help the Sextant," he added thoughtfully as he wandered away from her along one of the rows. "It could work for you, too. You could probably supply microgreens to half the restaurants in Portland, in New Hampshire, shoot, maybe even Boston. You could turn a tidy little profit. Help you pay for this nice greenhouse." Damon glanced over at her as he rounded the end of the bench.

"What makes you think I need help?"

He tapped a hanging basket with his fingertips as he walked, setting it swinging. "I know it's new, and judging by the look of your truck, you're not exactly rolling in dough." He pushed another basket so it swayed. "And for a person who's running a business, you sure seem to spend a lot more time around here than you do on job sites."

"I didn't realize you were paying such close attention," she returned tartly, reaching for more petunias to transplant.

"I always pay attention." He nudged the next basket in line to sway with the rest. "Especially to people who interest me."

"Or to people who can do things for you."

"Or in your case, both." He came up short in front of her. "I find myself thinking about you, Cady McBain, a lot. Why is that?"

"You're bored." She would have backed up but the wood of the workbench was behind her. "You're stuck in a small town."

"It's not boredom."

"And it's not about me." She tried for dismissive but her voice came out oddly breathless.

"Oh, I think it's very definitely about you. I keep finding myself wondering what it would be like to kiss you. I'm cutting up fruit and I'm wondering about the way you taste, about the way you always smell like apples and cinnamon." He rested his hands against the bench on either side of her, trapping her. "When you've got a job that involves sharp knives, spending a lot of time wondering isn't very healthy."

Any reply she might have made dried up in her throat. He stood before her, his face a study in lines and planes. The ruddy glow of the afternoon sun coming through the greenhouse walls turned his skin golden, like that of some herald in an old painting. His eyes were hot and dark on hers.

"You know this doesn't make sense," she said unsteadily.

"Probably not, but we're both wondering about it." He moved in, stepping between her feet.

"I'm not your type."

His fingers slipped into her hair. "I'd say that's for me to decide."

"You're not my type."

"I think I can change your mind," he whispered. And then his mouth came down on hers.

If he'd been gentle, she might have been able to ward him off. Perhaps he realized that, because he gave her no chance to think, just dragged them both into the kiss.

Heat. Friction. The warmth of mouth, the slick of tongue. The pleasure burst through her in a furious blend of taste and texture until it was all she could focus on. He kissed her as though he owned her, as though he'd watched her and learned every nuance of her. She had no defense for it, no way to hold back, and even if she had she was too dazed to want to. The hand she'd pressed against his chest to stop him curled into the fabric of his tunic, because she was suddenly afraid that if she didn't hold on, she might go spinning away into a hot madness.

Cady had kissed guys before. She'd always figured it wasn't a big deal; she knew what it was about. She knew nothing, she realized as she tasted Damon, inhaled the scent of him, felt the brush of the stubble on his chin.

And she wanted more.

He'd kissed her because he'd been curious, because he was tired and more than a bit annoyed at having her on his mind. It stung his pride to be preoccupied with a woman who claimed to be indifferent to him. But when he heard that soft gasp of pleasure, felt her finally surrender and slide her arms around him, it wasn't about annoyance or curiosity.

It was about desire, pure and simple.

He'd expected a quick, matter-of-fact kiss that would satisfy his curiosity. He hadn't expected her to be soft and yielding against him. He hadn't expected that apple-cinnamon scent of hers to wind into his senses and make him dizzy. He hadn't expected her to give.

He hadn't expected her to drive every other thought out of his head.

When he raised his head, it was for the sake of his own sanity.

Stunned, Cady stared back at him. Her eyes were huge and dark. Her mouth was swollen from his.

Abruptly, he felt annoyed with himself even as he wanted more. This wasn't what he was supposed to be doing here. He'd come to Maine to change.

Suddenly, change didn't seem all that appealing.

She shifted away from him, eyes clearing. Perversely, it gave him the urge to hold her tighter. Instead, he made himself release her.

She paced a few steps from him as though seeking safety. "Happy? Satisfied your curiosity?"

"Not by half." His irritation rose a notch because he realized it was true.

"Too bad, because that's it." But her lips still felt hot and bruised from his. He'd kissed her as no one had ever kissed her. He'd woken up every sleeping desire she'd ever had. He'd made her yearn, and that scared the hell out of her.

Because she knew it wasn't real.

"That's it?" he repeated and started back toward her. "I

don't think so. I don't know what's going on here but you don't start up something like this and just shut it down."

"I wasn't the one who started it," she retorted.

"But you were part of it. And you kissed me back, you can't pretend you didn't."

Cady could feel her cheeks heat. "So you're a good kisser, big deal. You ought to be, after all the practice you've had."

Her jab didn't make him angry, as she'd hoped. His slow smile was far more dangerous. "Practice has made me good at a lot of things. Want me to show you?"

"No." It was too quick and a little too nervous sounding. It took all she had not to move away as he stopped before her and leaned in by her ear.

"It happened," he murmured. "You can't make it go away. Maybe it's not smart but you and I both know we're going to be thinking about it until the next time."

And turning, he left her there, shaking.

Chapter Six

It was difficult, Cady discovered, to avoid thinking about someone when the person you were trying to avoid thinking about was always around. It was even worse when they popped up in your dreams. She could try all she wanted to forget; she could tell herself she wanted no part of him.

She couldn't stop thinking about the kiss.

She'd always told herself she was different, worn it like a badge of honor, but when she remembered the feel of his mouth on hers, her legs got weak. And that was no way to be feeling with the leg weakener nearby.

She knelt at one of the flower beds on the back side of the inn, setting out marigolds as quickly as she could. Behind her, closer than she liked, lay the restaurant. And Damon. She'd put off planting this particular bed as long as she could. Now, she flipped a pony pack over in her hand, hurrying to finish. The last thing she wanted to do was to run into him, with that low, persuasive voice and that killer smile.

The worst part of it was that she couldn't really blame the kiss on his smile. She could have stopped him if she'd really wanted to. She hadn't. He'd been right that day in the greenhouse; they'd both been wondering about it. And if she'd been awash in nerves when he'd approached, she'd been awash in anticipation, too.

Making a noise of frustration, Cady picked up another pony pack. The problem was that her workdays were largely physical. Normally, that suited her to a T because she was largely physical, too. Now, though, it merely provided her with way too much time to think.

About Damon. About the kiss. And about all of the other things she was missing.

Her hands slowed. What would it be like to have him touch her, really touch her? What would it be like to have those strong, nimble hands on her skin? She'd had so little experience—kisses with a few men, a pair of memorably disappointing encounters in bed. How would it be with a man who knew about pleasure? And if he could take her so far with a kiss, what else could he do?

The back of her neck prickled and she reached back to rub it absently. Bad question to ask. It was pointless—dangerous, more like—to think about sex or anything else with Damon Hurst. Like a deer trying to have a relationship with a hunter, and she wasn't the one wearing the camouflage vest. He was here and gone, and she needed to remember that.

Cady rubbed her neck again and shifted uneasily. The prickling hadn't gone away. Even though it was a cloudy day, even though she was working under the shade of the tall pines that grew between inn and restaurant, the back of her neck felt hot.

Just her imagination, Cady told herself. But she couldn't keep from glancing over her shoulder.

Only to see Damon in his apron, leaning idly against the wall by the back door. He looked tall, lean, insouciant. His teeth flashed white as he tapped the side of his fingers to his forehead in a mock salute. Face flaming, she turned hastily back to her marigolds.

It had been going like that all week. The more she tried to avoid him, the more he was everywhere she looked. No matter how early she dropped in to work the grounds or tend the greenhouse or get supplies for her workday, she always seemed to run into him. He'd be heading into work or coming back from the farmers' market or taking a break from the heat of the kitchen, but he'd be there.

The fact that she'd been able to avoid talking to him so far was scant comfort. She could read it in his eyes as he nodded or winked or gave one of those half-assed salutes: he hadn't forgotten. He was just biding his time.

The thought made her stomach tighten.

Enough, she thought impatiently and pressed another marigold into place, using her knuckles to tamp down the earth around each plant. She didn't need to think about it anymore. What she needed to do was—

A thump and a curse from one of the guesthouses had her glancing over. It was her father, carrying one of the inn's Adirondack chairs up the stairs to the guesthouse deck, and not having an easy time of it.

She frowned as he stopped halfway up, leaning on the railing, breathing hard. "Dad?" she called, rising to her feet. "You want some help?"

She didn't wait for the answer but jogged over anyway. By the time she got there, he was standing again and waving her away. "Everything's fine, hon. I was just catching my breath. This fool cold I've had just won't go away." He wiped his forehead.

She caught hold of the bottom of the chair and began carrying it up with him. "Don't you have someone who can do this?" She shook her head before the words were even out.

"Okay, dumb question, never mind. But seriously, maybe you ought to give it a rest. You don't look so hot."

"I'm fine," he puffed. "I just need to kick this bug."

"You just need to stop running yourself into the ground," she countered. "Didn't the doctor tell you that last week?"

"The doctor's office is probably where I got the cold. I was fine until I went to see him."

"You probably had it already, you just didn't have symptoms."

"That's what your mother says."

"And if you don't take care of yourself, you'll never get over it," Cady scolded.

"Your mother says that, too."

"Lucky you, surrounded by adoring women."

"Or women who think they're always right."

"That's because we are right," she said as they topped the stairs. "And one thing I'm right about is that you need to take a break."

"I'd better not. I've got to get these chairs out. Tomorrow's Friday and we're full up. First time all year." He sank down on the Adirondack with a sigh. "I just need to sit down for a minute, that's all."

"What you need is to take some ibuprofen and go to bed." She bent over him worriedly, studying his pasty face. "I'm going to call Tucker. He and I can put the chairs out."

"Don't bother him," Ian protested. "He's got the marina to worry about."

"I'll help him push his boats around next week." Straightening, she pulled out her cell phone.

Ring tones sounded in her ear and then there was a click. "Whadda you want?" Tucker demanded, but she could hear the grin in his voice.

"Is that any way to talk to your favorite cousin?" Cady asked.

"The one who never calls me unless she wants to ask a favor? That cousin?"

"You mean the cousin who comes to every one of your gigs, no matter how many Dave Matthews songs you insist on playing?" Tucker played bass on weekends in a local bar band that featured more enthusiasm than talent.

He gave an elaborate sigh. "All right, all right. What is it this time?"

"I need your help moving some deck furniture. Dad's not feeling so good."

"I'm feeling fine," Ian muttered bad-temperedly.

"He's not feeling so good," she repeated. "There isn't that much to move. We could probably do it in half an hour if you've got the time."

"Be there in five," Tucker responded without hesitation, hanging up. Over on the docks, she could see him leaving the marina kiosk in his work shirt and jeans.

"Everything all right?" a voice called and she glanced down to see Damon at the foot of the stairs.

Any nerves she might have felt were tamped down by concern. "Just calling in reinforcements," she told him. Behind her, Ian shifted. "Don't you move or I'll call Mom," she threatened, turning to give him a stare.

"Not one of you kids gives me any respect," Ian complained.

"I know. You're so maltreated," she soothed, leaning in to kiss his forehead. "Now be quiet and rest. Better yet, go back to the house and lie down."

"I can't do that. One of the waiters called in sick. I've got to fill in for him tonight and there's way too much to get done before then."

"You're not working anybody's shift. I'll take it."

Ian snorted. "You hate waiting tables more than you hate working the front desk."

"What doesn't kill me makes me stronger." She flashed him a grin before turning for the stairs. "Besides, I can use the tips."

Damon was waiting for her when she reached the bottom. "He okay?"

Her smile faded. "Just a cold that's coming back," she said. "He tries to do too much sometimes. It happens when your job description includes everything."

Damon glanced over at the array of slatted wooden chairs and snack tables outside the storage shed. "Where are all those going?"

"On the decks of the guesthouses."

"Lotta stairs," he observed.

"You've noticed that?"

"I guess maybe you could use some help."

"Speaking of jobs, shouldn't you be in slinging hash?"

"I get time off for good behavior," he told her.

"I'll skip pointing out the obvious because we need to get these chairs out," she said. "If you're serious about the offer, we need two chairs on each deck, plus a snack table."

"You outsourcing my job?" Tucker demanded from behind her.

Cady rolled her eyes. "In case you two haven't met, Damon, this is my cousin Tucker McBain, who runs the marina. Tucker, this is Damon Hurst, the new chef at the restaurant."

Tucker had sun-streaked brown hair and the easy grin of a man who spent his life on the water he loved. He also had the McBain height that only Cady had somehow missed inheriting. It gave him an appearance of lankiness that was deceptive; a person who looked carefully would see the muscle and power Tucker had developed over years of running the marina and working his lines of lobster pots. A person who underestimated him would be both foolish and sorry.

"Now she's raiding the kitchen for conscript labor." Tucker shook hands with Damon. "She's out of control."

"Clearly."

"So, you in on this gig?"

"Long as we finish it before dinner service starts," Damon said.

"We'd better finish earlier than that," Cady told them. "I have to go change."

Tucker raised a brow. "Jeans and a T-shirt not dressy enough for planting flowers?"

She wrinkled her nose at him. "I've got to fill in for one of the waiters during dinner tonight."

The two men stared. "You?" Damon asked.

"What about me?"

"Well, getting let loose on the unsuspecting general public, for one."

Her brows drew down. "Hey, it's either me or Dad and he looks to me like he needs the night off."

"Uncle Ian knows about this?" Tucker shook his head. "He must be sick if he's agreed."

"Can we just move the chairs, please?" Cady muttered.

Tucker grabbed a chair and hoisted it with a grunt. "What the hell are these things made of, iron?"

"Teak," Cady supplied. "It's heavy."

"No kidding."

"Okay," she said, "I'll take the chairs for guesthouse one, you guys can get guesthouse two."

Tucker eyed Damon. "She likes to run things."

"So I've noticed."

Ignoring them, Cady carried a chair toward the stairs of a guesthouse. She stopped at the bottom step, eyeing the treads.

"Overambitious, too," said Tucker, stepping around her with the chair he carried.

"Yep. And permanently cranky," Damon added, neatly lifting the Adirondack out of Cady's hands, ignoring her squawk of protest.

"You're a good judge of character," Tucker approved as they began climbing the stairs.

"It doesn't take a genius and it doesn't take long," Damon said.

"You can talk about me like I'm actually here, you know." Cady's voice was testy as she carried up the little drinks table. "And I didn't need you to carry that chair for me."

"You hear something?" Damon asked Tucker.

"Probably the wind in the trees." Tucker reached the deck and set down his chair with a sigh of relief.

"Wind from somewhere," Damon added.

"Funny, guys," Cady said, scowling. "How'd you get to be so funny?"

"Just natural talent," Tucker said modestly.

Chapter Seven

Hauling furniture wouldn't have been his choice of a way to spend a couple of hours, Damon thought as he fired entrées for the staff meal, but all things considered, it hadn't been bad. Not that he was happy to see Ian McBain sick, but schlepping chairs had been a good excuse to be outside.

And to spend time with Cady.

He'd kept his distance after that afternoon in the greenhouse, in part to give her space, in part to give himself time to get his head together. He was supposed to be walking the straight and narrow now, not turning around to make the same mistakes with the same kinds of people. But Cady wasn't quite like anybody he could think of, and he wasn't at all sure that she was a mistake.

He finished up another plate and slid it across the steel counter under the overhead shelf to the pass where waiters picked up plates. The servers were beginning to crowd around like cats at the sound of a can opener. Even as they were filling the butter dishes for the bread baskets and topping off salt, pepper and cream containers, they could smell the food. They knew the staff meal was near.

Staff meal or family meal was traditionally a haphazard exercise in turning leftovers and scraps not fit for diners into something vaguely edible to keep floor and kitchen staff going through service. Damon had never subscribed to that approach, though. In France, Descour had always served family meal at the table, with plates and napkins and real food. Treat the staff right and they'll treat the customers right, was his theory. A good one. And Damon had carried it out ever since.

Of course, that didn't mean that family meal couldn't double as the waiters' meeting and tasting. Especially now, when he was shifting the old menu over to the new one by a half-dozen dishes a night. The servers needed to taste the new entrées and appetizers, see how to place them on the table, know the ingredients and presentation so they could answer questions, if necessary.

With a quick flick of the wrist, he drizzled brilliant green chive oil around the last plate and pushed it over to the pass. "Okay, listen up, people. We're still in the process of changing over the menu. Tonight, we're launching the new seafood—"

And then Cady walked in and his train of thought didn't just derail. It went right off the damned trestle.

He'd seen her already that day, watched her in her worn jeans and T-shirt as she'd planted flowers, moved furniture. Watched her and tried not to remember how she'd felt in his arms. But the woman who walked in wearing the uniform of white tuxedo jacket and narrow black skirt bore no resemblance to that Cady at all.

Slender, he'd no idea she was so slender. Perhaps it was the formal clothing, but she looked graceful, taller somehow. The skirt was far from short, almost demure, and yet it seemed almost indecent as it revealed a pair of startlingly lovely legs. She'd drawn her hair back with combs. There was a delicacy to her face, he saw now, one he'd never fully appreciated. Her mouth looked soft and tempting beyond all sense.

She'd kissed him with those lips, kissed him and gasped against him and spun his world right around. And though he could tell himself that he shouldn't have done it, he wasn't a damned bit sorry. And, he realized, he had every intention of doing it again.

Regardless of the consequences.

He cleared his throat. "Right. Let's talk about the new entrées for tonight."

You didn't grow up around an inn like the Compass Rose without learning every aspect of the business—whether you wanted to or not. Working in the restaurant might have been Cady's least favorite activity, but she'd bussed and even waited tables from the time she'd been sixteen.

So she put on the white shirt and bow tie and the tuxedo jacket in preparation for her shift. If she added lipstick and actually took a few minutes to fuss with her hair, it had nothing to do with seeing Damon. She was merely being professional, she told herself, nerves roiling her stomach as she walked into the kitchen. But the little buzz of purely female satisfaction she felt when he gave her the double take had nothing to do with professionalism.

It was strictly personal.

Given her choice, Cady would have skipped family meal. Showing up two hours before the start of dinner service ate up precious time and she didn't trust herself around Damon any more than was absolutely necessary. Her parents had insisted, though. And now, as she stood at the end of the line and stared at the plates, she understood why.

Things had changed—the menu, for one. Gone were many

of the dishes that the Sextant had served for decades. Those that remained had been reinterpreted—the baked New England dinner of seafood covered in bread crumbs had morphed into pan-seared scallops with brioche minicroutons and lemon beurre blanc, for example. And to the delight of the servers, Damon was serving the plates for family meal.

Fancy plates, Cady saw, arranged like sculptures, painted with color. Pretty enough, but it was the incredible smell wafting up from them that had her mouth watering. Of course, it had the same effect on the crowd of floor staff currently digging in with forks and knives.

"Alfred, for chrissakes, that was my hand, not the veal," complained a tall blonde named Sylvia.

"And here I was going to tell Chef that the meat wasn't tender," stocky Alfred returned, shoveling a bite of roasted potatoes into his mouth. "Now I understand."

Amused, Cady looked up, only to catch the eye of the chef in question.

"I knew you couldn't stay away," Damon singsonged under his breath as he walked past her to the line.

"I'm only here because I'm working," she shot back.

"Well, if you're going to be working, you'd better get in there and try the entrées. How else are you going to be able to answer questions?"

"No thanks," she said, glancing over at the clutch of waiters. "I'd like to keep my fingers just the way they are."

Damon turned to the oven behind him and pulled out a ramekin. He pushed it over to Cady. "Here."

She poked at it suspiciously with a fork. "What is it?"

"Something I made special when I heard you were coming. Fresh-made penne with a truffled asiago and fontina béchamel." His lips twitched at her blank stare. "Macaroni and cheese."

Tentatively, Cady took a forkful, and put it into her mouth.

And pure bliss flooded through her. Tangy cheese, silky cream, an addictive hint of earthiness. "Oh my God," she mumbled, reaching out for more. "This is incredible." In the midst of taking another bite, she glanced over at Damon.

And felt a flare of heat that had nothing to do with the food.

He was watching her again with that naked hunger in his eyes. She held the fork but he was the one who looked starved—and she was the main course. He stepped closer to her, his gaze never wavering.

"You think I can make your mouth happy now," he murmured into her ear, "just wait."

She swallowed. "Dream on."

"Remind me to tell you what's been happening in my dreams lately," he said softly. "I think you'll find it very interesting."

There were glints of gold in those dark eyes, she realized as she stared back helplessly, like sparks at midnight. And his mouth had been so soft. Nearby, the rest of the staff were oblivious, but the feeding frenzy was beginning to die down. She moistened her lips. "This isn't the place or the time."

"Give me another place and another time, then."

"Later," was the best she could do. "Right now, we need to worry about dinner service."

"And later we'll worry about something else."

The dining room, with its broad sweep of windows looking out over Grace Harbor, had always been one of her favorite places at the inn. Antique maps of the Maine Coast dotted the pale blue walls, rugs covered the wide-planked maple floors. Atop each snowy-white tablecloth sat a glass storm lantern with a flickering candle. Outside, the sailboats in the marina bobbed on water stained gold by the last rays of the setting sun.

It had been a while since she'd waited tables. She'd forgotten just how exhausting it could be. By the end of the first hour, she'd discovered that her new black shoes pinched; by the second, she'd managed to punch a hole in her finger with the corkscrew. By the third, her arms were leaden from carrying heavy plates.

It could've been worse—at least the servers didn't have to haul the meals from kitchen to table. That honor fell to the runners, who carted the heavy trays of dishes out to a station in the dining room where Cady and the other waiters delivered them to waiting diners. Not that the arrangement had kept her from burning herself on a plate that had been broiled under the salamander a little too long. All things considered, though, she'd probably gotten off easy.

"Waitress, over here."

Or maybe not.

She turned to see a disgruntled-looking man waving at her from a table in the corner. The flesh of his neck spilled over his collar; his comb-over didn't hide the pink shine of his scalp. The hint of embarrassment in the face of his companion across the table warned Cady that it wasn't his incipient baldness that had made him unhappy, though.

She gave him her best smile. "How are your meals?" she asked.

"Terrible." The man's face was dark with displeasure.

"What seems to be the problem?"

"I ordered fois gras glazed tenderloin, medium well. It's not glazed, it's all dried out, including the meat."

Cady glanced at the plate. "It looks right to me, sir. That's the way the dish is made."

"Well, that's not the way it sounds from the description. You can't serve meat dry like this. It needs some kind of a sauce."

Perfect. Cady could just imagine walking into the kitchen and delivering that particular bit of news to Damon. She'd wind up with the plate launched at her head, if she weren't careful. Or the customer tossed into the parking lot.

"I think it's dry because you asked for medium well, sir. I

did warn you that this cut of meat is very difficult to cook anywhere past medium. The chef recommends that if you want something more well-done, you order the rib eye."

"If I'd wanted the rib eye, I would have ordered the rib eye," he said peevishly. "I *ordered* the tenderloin."

"But, sir—"

"No buts. I want it sent back."

"Walter." His companion looked embarrassed.

"I want my dinner," he returned, obstinacy in the very set of his shoulders.

Cady sighed. "I'll take it back, sir. It'll just be a few minutes."

Now this, she thought, had all the makings of a disaster.

During one renovation or other, a McBain had installed a double set of sliding doors between the dining room and the kitchen, separated by a vestibule. The arrangement insulated the dining room from the racket of the kitchen. It also gave Cady brief refuge before facing Damon with the unwelcome news that a customer had had the temerity to suggest that not only had they overcooked the tenderloin but that the very concept of the dish was faulty.

She took a deep breath and walked through the second set of doors.

The unbroken hot surface of the stove was festooned with steaming kettles of soup and boiling pasta water and what looked like dozens of sauté pans of sizzling meat and fish. On a shelf above the stovetop, dozens more clean sauté pans sat waiting, flanked on either end by salamanders for warming finished plates or adding a final broil.

In the lane between the stove line and the counter stood the trio of white-aproned line chefs. At the far end, quick-handed Roman manned the grill and deep fryer; in the middle was Rosalie, on veg and pasta; and nearest Cady, on sauté, stood Damon.

During Nathan's tenure, the scene had been one of more

than a little chaos, with insults and ribald jokes flying thick and fast above the sound of speed metal from the radio. Now, the room was almost eerily quiet. Gone was the music, gone was the sense of untidy confusion. In its place was a focused calm. The only voices were those of the expediter, Andy, reading off the orders as they printed out on the machine in the corner, and Damon repeating them.

The printer chattered. "One tenderloin, one salmon, two lobster," Andy called out.

"One tenderloin, one salmon, two lobster," Damon echoed.

Watching the group at work was a bit like watching a ballet because for all the quiet, the line was the scene of rapid, purposeful activity so synchronized it could have been choreographed. The cooks pivoted between stove and counter, passing plates to one another, saucing and garnishing, each of them working on three and four dishes simultaneously.

And as in a ballet, there was always one who was impossible to stop watching. Damon worked the end of the line in constant motion, bending, reaching, flipping, stirring, shaking a sauté pan with one hand while seasoning an entrée with the other. And, she swore, plating up with a third. There was a precision to his movements and more than a little grace, as though he were indeed going through the moves of a dance. He seemed totally absorbed in the process, bending over every plate as he worked with a swift, silent, almost ferocious concentration.

"Two scallop, veal medium rare, rib eye well," Andy called out.

"Two scallop, veal medium rare, rib eye dead." Damon reached to the shelf above the stove line for a trio of sauté pans, setting them on the stove to heat.

"One rib eye dead," echoed Roman with a grin, slapping the cut on the grill.

Grabbing a cylindrical bain-marie from its simmering water bath, Damon ladled a sauce into a fourth pan and put it on a back burner to reduce. "Where are we at on table ten?" he asked, moving a sizzling pan of what looked like tenderloin from stovetop to oven.

"Ready on the rib eye, one salmon in the salamander, one on the grill," Roman responded.

"Risotto's done. One minute on the lobsters," put in Rosalie, winding pasta around a meat fork to provide a bed for one of her lobster tails.

By the time she'd finished speaking, Damon had the veal seasoned and into the pan with the shallots to sear off. "Okay, stop where you are on the last order. Let's focus on getting this eight-top out." Reaching into one of the ovens, he pulled out two sauté pans, each with a piece of meat that was finished cooking. Lamb loin, Cady recognized.

He flipped the meat onto the cutting board and deftly sliced each loin into medallions, leaving them together like a sideways stack of poker chips. Even as he reached out, Rosalie passed him a pair of plates with mashed potatoes piled in one corner. He pulled a bubbling sauté pan of what looked like wine sauce from the stove and drizzled a circle onto each plate, then used his knife to lay the stack of medallions in the middle, pressing them gently over so that the perfect rounds of lamb lay against one another in the ring of red.

"Veg, Rosalie," he said, sliding over the two plates so she could add the tiniest zucchini and yellow squash Cady had ever seen. Meanwhile, Rosalie had traded him her two lobster plates. With a squeeze bottle, he added a few precise dots of lemon butter sauce around the edges of each, adhering to some vision that only he could see.

Meanwhile, Andy the expediter was madly sprinkling sliver-thin parsley chiffonade over the lamb and risotto and sticking what looked suspiciously like fancy potato chips into the top of the mashed potatoes. He and Damon slid the plates across the counter to the pass.

Less than a minute had elapsed.

"All right, table ten up," Damon called. "Let's go, people. Hands on hot food." He clapped his hands. The runners swarmed in.

Cady cleared her throat. "Chef?" she said.

Damon turned from adding knobs of butter to two of his sauté pans. He started to flash a smile. Until he saw the plate in her hands. "What's that?"

"Fois gras glazed tenderloin from table four."

"I can see that." He flipped the veal. "The question is what is it doing back in the kitchen?"

This was the delicate part, she thought. Little was more irritating to a chef than having to interrupt the complicated dance of getting orders out the door to redo a plate he'd thought was safely gone. And when that chef was Damon Hurst, almost anything could happen.

"The customer isn't happy. He says it's too dry. He wants a sauce."

Damon's eyes narrowed. "Table four, that was medium well, right?"

Cady nodded.

"Well, yeah, it's dry. It's been cooked to death."

"I tried to suggest the rib eye, but he didn't want to hear it."

"Roman, toss this one in the Frialator," Damon directed, slapping a new piece of tenderloin onto a sizzle platter and sliding it down the counter as if he were playing kitchen shuffleboard. "Set phasers for medium well."

"Aye, aye, Captain." Roman grinned.

Damon turned back to the stove to get the veal in the oven and add scallops to the other two sauté pans. "Now what's his sauce issue?"

"He says when he saw glazed, he wasn't expecting a crust," Cady said.

"Did you tell him that's how the dish is made?"

"He didn't want to listen to me."

"Maybe he'll listen to me," Damon said with an edge to his voice.

The printer chattered. "Three lobster, one scallop, two tenderloin medium, one lamb rare," Andy read.

"I don't really think—"

"I've got to get some entrées plated," Damon interrupted.

"But what do I tell him?" Cady asked desperately.

"Leave it to me. I know how to handle these kinds of idiots. Now go take care of your tables." He turned away, hands already moving in a blur.

Chapter Eight

Cady went back out to the dining room, mind buzzing. On the positive side, he hadn't actually gone ballistic. That was a good sign, wasn't it? If he'd planned to kick them out, wouldn't he have stormed into the dining room?

Leave it to me. I know how to handle these kinds of idiots.

He'd looked well and truly ticked. And no matter how she tried to respin what he'd said, it didn't sound good. She'd seen it before on camera, seen that intensity flare into scorching temper.

Well, it wasn't going to happen here. Clamping her jaw tight, she headed for the kitchen just as Damon strode out. She moved to intercept him. "Don't even think about it."

"Think about what?" he asked without stopping.

"Kicking him out." Cady followed hot on his heels.

"It sounds to me like he's got it coming."

"My parents don't."

"Leave this to me," he told her. "I'll deal with it."

That was what she was afraid of. With every minute Damon was out of the kitchen, the line fell further and further behind. He wouldn't be in the dining room unless he was planning something.

The part of her that had been predicting disaster should have felt unsurprised—vindicated, even—to see it all play out as she'd predicted. But, she suddenly realized, there was another part of her that had begun to hope for something different. There was another part of her that had begun to believe things had changed.

"You are not going to make a scene," she hissed, seizing his arm to tug him behind the high barrier of the empty waiters' station. "Don't you dare kick him out."

"Why not?" He stepped toward her, backing her into the wood of the barrier. "Give me a good reason not to, just one."

She could hear the suppressed anger in his voice and she knew suddenly he wasn't talking about a dissatisfied customer.

Dark eyes, simmering intensity, a stare that didn't ask but demanded. Her hand fell away from his arm as she breathed in slowly. "This isn't the—"

"Time or place." Damon caught her wrists. "You say that a lot. You ask me, it's long past the time and place."

A treacherous weakness began to seep through her. "Not here," she said desperately.

"Then where? When?"

"Later, all right?"

"At the end of the night?"

"Whatever you want, just don't—"

"Good." And he turned toward the table before she could catch him.

"Good evening," he said to the couple, inclining his head. "I'm your chef, Damon Hurst. I hear you're not happy with your meal."

"It was terrible," the balding man grumped. "Poorly cooked, not what the menu promised."

"I see." She could see the tension in Damon's shoulders.

"What do you intend to do about it?"

Here it came, Cady thought, and stepped forward. "Damon, we—"

"I've made you a new entrée." Damon nodded to a runner who set a fresh plate before the man.

"What about my wife? Her dinner's stone-cold by now."

"Walter, it's not a problem," the woman began.

"I thought that might happen," Damon said, even as the runner whisked her plate away and set down another.

Cady gaped.

"What is this?" The man poked at the meat on his plate.

"Beef tenderloin with a truffled fois gras sauce I whipped up," Damon told him. "It's got a bit of wine, some caramelized shallots."

The man took a bite and chewed. "Huh." He chewed some more. "It's good." Swiftly, he cut another piece. "Really good. Isabel, you've got to try this."

But Isabel wasn't listening. She was staring at Damon. "Damon Hurst," she said slowly as though just registering the words. "You're that chef, aren't you? The one on TV?"

"Now and then," he said.

"Oh, I love your show. I can't believe we've had your food. The girls in my bridge club will be so jealous."

"I'm here Tuesday through Saturday. Tell them to come in. What's your name?"

"Isabel Cottler," she supplied. "This is my husband, Walter."

"Isabel, tell your friends to give the waiter your name when they come. I'll take special care of them."

"Oh!" She pinkened. "I will, you can be sure. Thank you so much."

"No, thank you."

Stunned, Cady watched as he sketched a small bow and left them to their dinners.

"What happened to the guy who used to throw customers out into the street?" she asked as she followed him back to the kitchen.

"Who wants to be predictable?" He stopped in the vestibule and turned to her. "Besides, I got something out of it."

Her pulse bumped. "What I said doesn't count. You plated new entrées. You were never planning to kick them out."

"We made a bargain."

"I have to go check my tables," she retorted.

But before she could escape, he leaned in and brushed his lips over hers. "You do that. I'll see you when service is through." And he stepped through the doors into the kitchen, leaving her standing there.

The final hours of dinner service passed by in a blur of taking orders, delivering plates, opening wine. When Cady saw the last customers rise to leave, she should have felt relief at the prospect of release. Instead, she just felt disoriented.

Damon. She didn't know what to think. Nothing about him was as she'd expected. Instead of partying into the wee hours and showing up at work in the late afternoon, he was in the kitchen at the crack of dawn every morning. Instead of shouting at his staff, he presided over a kitchen that was positively serene. Instead of kicking out rude customers, he charmed them.

And somehow, when she hadn't been paying attention, he'd charmed her.

She'd agreed to something in those desperate moments in the dining room, though she wasn't sure what. And she wasn't at all sure how she felt about it. Nerves, yes. Anticipation, yes. And confusion. She didn't like confusion, she never had, and so she took her time with her after-hours duties, changing tablecloths, refilling salt cellars, putting off heading to the kitchen to the last possible moment.

She couldn't say whether it was relief or disappointment that hit when she finally walked through the sliding doors only to find the kitchen cleared out. The rest of the floor staff was long gone, the line cooks had finished cleaning up and headed to the locker room to change. Only Denny, the kitchen porter, remained for the thankless job of washing the mountain of dishes and pans, taking out the rubbish, mopping the floors and counters for the new day.

Damon was nowhere to be found.

Which was good news. Definitely good news, she thought as she retrieved her keys and jacket from the now-empty locker room and slammed bad-temperedly out the back door. A woman would be out of her mind to take the risk of getting involved with Damon Hurst, with that mind-melting stare that could make her think she really wanted his kisses, wanted his touch, wanted his—

"It's about time."

Cady froze.

"I was beginning to wonder whether you were moving in." Damon stepped out of the shadows into the pool of light outside the door. He wore jeans and an open-collared paisley shirt under his leather jacket. With his hair loose, his jaw dark with a full day's growth, he looked like an artist who'd escaped his garret. The naked bulb overhead threw his eyes into shadow.

Nerves, anticipation, confusion. Cady swallowed. "I had things to do."

"We still do."

"You can't hold me to that. That was extortion."

"Hardly. You were free to say no."

Nerves, anticipation, confusion.

"You knew I thought you were going to kick them out."

"Maybe I meant to."

"After you'd already made up plates?"

"It doesn't matter," he said, watching her with that unwavering stare. "I think we have some unfinished business."

Nerves, anticipation, confusion.

Nerves won.

"It's twelve-thirty in the morning. I think the business can wait." And a part of her wasn't at all sure she could handle what that business might be. She started toward the parking area, tucked in pockets among the stands of pines that surrounded them.

And Damon walked beside her, through the shadows. "I didn't have you picked for the type who'd go back on her word."

She snapped her head around to stare at him in the dimness. "I'm not."

"So?"

"So this isn't the place to have some big talk. We both know there are too many people around."

"Fewer all the time," Damon observed as the last stragglers headed for the exit. "And who said I wanted to talk?"

The thick pines loomed around them, breaking the wash of illumination from the arc lamps into stripes of bright and dark. Their feet crunched on the pine needles underfoot. Then, with a flash of taillights, the final car drove away and they were alone.

Cady stopped at the side of her truck and turned to face him. Against her will, anticipation began to thrum inside her.

He fingered her bow tie. "You stopped me in my tracks tonight when I saw you."

"It's just the tuxedo."

When he looked her up and down, she felt his gaze as surely as any touch. "No," he said simply. "I'm pretty confident it's got nothing to do with the tux."

Her mouth went dry. He watched her with the same intensity as when he was at work, creating, but now it was all focused on her.

"Why didn't you make a scene with that diner tonight?" she asked. Abruptly, it seemed vital to know. "He was obnoxious. Why didn't you kick him out? It's what you would have done in New York."

Damon moved his shoulders. "This isn't New York."

"Is that why you don't party all night anymore?"

He reached out to tuck her hair behind her ear. "I can think of other things I'd rather do."

His fingers lingered against her cheek and Cady felt a flip in her stomach. It was only a light touch and yet she was trembling.

Nerves, anticipation, confusion.

"Why are you here?" she managed.

"To cook." He traced his fingers down the side of her throat. "That's what I do."

"You can do that anywhere."

"I'd rather do it here."

Cady moistened her lips, never taking her eyes from his. "I don't know what to think about you."

"Do you have to?"

It was imperative, somehow. But his hand was slipping back to curve around her neck, leaving a trail of heat that turned all her muscles liquid. She was sinking into lassitude and heat and wanting.

And wanting.

"I need to know," she murmured as he bent his head to hers. "I need…"

"What?" he whispered.

And then his mouth was on hers.

They had no business kissing out here in the parking lot where anyone could see them; Cady knew it but she couldn't make it matter. It wasn't the time, it wasn't the place, but the whole notion of right time and right place didn't seem important anymore. They could have been in a million different places at a million different times and still all she would have been able to register would be the heat of his mouth on hers.

He had a reputation as a volatile genius, as an unapologetic player. She'd never expected gentleness from him. Yet it was gentleness he gave; sweet, persuasive caresses that undermined her defenses and left her helpless to do anything but sink into the warmth and the pleasure.

And as she did, he took her deeper.

His mouth was soft on hers, his hands spread across her back to pull her to him. As he'd tempted her with his food, shown her a pleasure she'd never known she could experience, so he tempted her with his mouth. He teased her lips into parting, fastened his over hers as though they could give each other breath, sustenance.

But the taste of him, oh, the taste of him was far more addictive than anything he'd ever fed her, complex and intense and somehow wild. It was a flavor she could never forget. It was a taste she could never get enough of. More, she thought, and didn't know whether she meant the taste or the man.

Or both.

With a sound of impatience, she wound her fingers up into his hair and let her head fall back.

Damon could feel her, taut in his arms, could smell that apple-cinnamon scent. And he kissed his way across her cheek and down her throat, searching for the source of it.

He was a man who knew all about the appetite but there was no explanation for the desperate hunger he felt, and no answer to it. He tasted her skin, found himself maddened by the barrier of her clothing. The want for her drummed through him relentlessly.

Then he felt her shiver and it weakened him more than any fist in the gut could. She styled herself as tough, savvy, no-

nonsense, but here she was, trembling in his arms, her pulse beating frantically under his lips.

He'd been with dozens of women but it had never been like this. Cady, the things he was feeling, made any memories of any woman he'd ever known meaningless. The whispery little sigh of pleasure she gave made him tighten. He remembered how she'd looked when he'd fed her, that almost orgiastic expression of pleasure on her face. All he wanted was to give her more, take her further, slowly, while he was watching.

And go over the edge with her, together.

Desire burned away at his self-control. "I want you," he muttered.

I want you. Cady heard the words, felt Damon slipping his hands under her jacket, running them down her body and, oh, it felt delicious.

I want you. His mouth was back on hers, doing those wonderful, magical, mind-bending things and for a moment she melted against him, wanting only to glory in the feel of his hands but—

I want you. That meant sex and getting naked and nothing that had ever been any good for her. The thought made the dizzy pleasure dissolve away to reality. And then she was breaking the kiss, sucking in gulps of the cool night air.

The nerves were back.

What she was doing? she wondered, resting her forehead against his chest. He was used to women who knew what they were about, who weren't the least bit self-conscious, who knew all the ways to please a man. As to her, what little experience she'd had only reinforced one thing—that she hadn't a clue how to do it right. At least she didn't think so. She'd never been able to ask, in part because it was the one area in which her nerve failed her, and in part because she'd never gotten a chance for round two with either of the men she'd slept with.

It never occurred to her that the fault might not have been her own.

Damon slipped his fingers down to raise her chin. "What's wrong?"

"I just need to think." She moved away, because the heat of his body felt way too good and if she didn't watch it, she'd find herself browsing on his mouth again and begging for the feel of his hands. "I'm not... I don't date a lot. I don't know how it works, this hopping in and out of bed stuff. I'm not wired that way." And she was in over her head and feeling horribly self-conscious.

"I wasn't thinking too much about the hopping out part," he said.

"You know what I mean. I'm not one of these hip club chicks. I've never even been to Manhattan."

"I don't give a damn. You're who I want."

"Now, maybe."

He closed his eyes briefly. "More than you can possibly imagine."

"I'm not playing games with you. I just need to figure out what I'm doing." This was a first. Her body was screaming for more and she, the physical one, was worried about her head.

Or her heart.

She knew he wanted her, she'd felt the indisputable evidence. But what did that mean to him? Once, she would have been certain she'd known—and run like hell the other way. In the past two weeks, though, she'd seen an entirely different person. Did she trust that? Or did she trust all the stories she'd heard in the media? Who was he really? And could she risk herself to find out?

Damon walked a few feet away, hands on his hips. Somewhere out in the dark, a night creature rustled. It wasn't any louder than the sound of Cady's heartbeat in her ears.

Shaking his head, Damon turned back to her. "Look, if you

need time, you need time. I'm not going to lie and tell you that all I wanted from you tonight was talk. I want a lot more, and I think you do, too. But I can wait until you're sure." He looked at her a moment.

Cady hesitated. "I'm sorry. I'm not trying to—"

"I know. It's okay." He opened the door of her truck, watched her as she slid in. "Be careful driving home."

Her eyes were troubled. "I will." She started her engine and rolled down the window.

Damon rested his hands on the door. "You know, I've barely got today figured out. I don't know about tomorrow any more than you do. But I do know that you don't find this just anywhere. When you find a gift, you don't walk away from it. So take your time and figure things out. I'll be here."

He leaned in to brush a kiss over her lips. And stood there, watching her as she drove off into the night.

Chapter Nine

"Hello? Anyone home?" Cady walked in the door of her parents' house, on the back side of the Compass Rose property. The slate-blue Cape Cod had been built by her grandfather Malcolm right after he'd taken over the inn. It had allowed his family—and her own—to be immediately accessible to the inn without actually living in it. And every time she thought of the alternative of growing up on the other side of the wall from milling guests, Cady mentally blessed him.

"Hi, honey. What are you doing here?" Amanda walked through the doorway from the kitchen, rubbing on hand lotion.

"Breakfast." Cady raised up a bakery bag.

"I smell cinnamon rolls."

"And I smell coffee. Wanna trade?" Cady headed into the kitchen, glancing over her shoulder to her mother. "I came by to see how Dad was feeling."

"He got a good night's sleep last night, thanks to you."

Nice to know someone had, Cady thought wryly. "Is he feeling any better?"

"A little, maybe. He's over at the main house."

"Mom, it's six in the morning. What's he doing over there this early?"

"You know him. He feels guilty that he took off yesterday afternoon. I'm glad he did, though. He's been looking really run-down." Amanda poured coffee for her daughter and set it on the breakfast bar.

"You know, you guys do have staff. You could let them do some of the work for a change."

Amanda shook her head. "There's always some sort of crisis they don't know how to handle. You know how it is."

"I know how Dad is." Cady opened the bakery bag. "He thinks he's some kind of a machine that never gets sick and never needs to rest."

"He knows he's not." Amanda leaned against the counter to look across at her daughter.

"Then why does he want to run himself into the ground? He needs to start taking care of himself."

"He does what he thinks he needs to do."

"Sometimes I think you guys don't own the inn, the inn owns you." Cady dumped several heaping spoonfuls of sugar in her coffee and stirred.

"You're going to rot your teeth if you keep that up," Amanda said mildly.

"I brush them all the time." Cady took a bite of her cinnamon roll and followed it with a swallow of coffee. "I'm self-insured. Can't afford to have my premiums go up."

"And you're a small business owner, so you should know the business always owns you."

"Yeah, but my business doesn't require me to work around the clock." She stopped. "I worry about you guys. You don't have any backup so you just never take a rest."

Amanda turned to stare out the kitchen window at the inn, and Grace Harbor beyond. "That's nothing new. It's pretty much been that way since your grandfather retired. Before that, we had four of us to share the load. Everybody got days off. Since then…"

And Cady felt the familiar wash of guilt. "Mom, I'm sorry. I wish I could do more."

"Do more? You already do plenty." Amanda turned back to her. "Anyway, it's not your responsibility. It's not the responsibility of any of you kids. I mean, we would've been thrilled if any of you had wanted to run the inn, but you have your own lives to lead. We understand that."

"And you have your lives to lead, too. You used to talk about travel, seeing Europe and Asia."

"I watch the Travel Channel," Amanda said with a half smile.

"Maybe you should do more." Cady hesitated. "Maybe it's time for you guys to retire."

"You mean sell off."

"We're having Dad's sixtieth birthday party in two weeks," she said carefully. "I think maybe it's time."

"This inn has been in your father's family for almost a hundred years. It would break his heart to sell it."

"But, Mom, who's going to run it? Not Max. Certainly not Walker. I love the inn as much as you do. I just hate to see it turn into a millstone around your neck." The hellish part was, Cady knew the answer. She just didn't know if she could live with it. When it came to family, though, you did what you had to do. She took a deep breath. "You know, I've been thinking. Maybe I could—"

"No, honey." Amanda cut her off. "You do a beautiful job with the grounds, but there's no way you could run this place, if that's what you're thinking. You'd be miserable. And, well, as much as I love you, you'd be miserable at it. No offense."

"None taken," Cady returned grumpily.

Amanda came around the counter to hug her. "It was sweet of you to offer and I know what it cost. Don't worry. We'll figure something out." She turned to study Cady's cinnamon roll. "You know, my hips don't need one of those but my mouth just might."

Cady passed her a napkin. "You ask me, guilt is a waste of time."

"I had no idea I had such a wise daughter. Your mama must have raised you right."

"Absolutely."

"Thanks again for helping your father with the furniture and pitching in at the restaurant." Amanda perched on one of the kitchen stools. "How did everything go, by the way? What did you think of Damon in action?"

He kisses better than any man I've ever laid lips on.

"He's good," Cady said aloud. "His food's amazing. He keeps the kitchen running smooth as silk."

Too bad the same couldn't be said for her pulse when she was around him.

"Roman really seems to like him," Amanda said.

"Well, Roman ought to know." Cady set her coffee mug down and took a deep breath. "As much as I hate to admit it, I think I might have been wrong about him."

Amanda blinked. "You're not coming down with your father's cold, are you? You're looking a little puny, now that I think about it."

She wasn't coming down with her father's cold, but she was very worried that she was starting to come down with something else. "I'm fine." Cady brushed the concern aside. "I just didn't sleep so well last night."

"Why not? After a night on your feet waiting tables, I would've thought you would have slept like a rock."

If rocks tossed and turned and spent the whole night thinking of a man with a hypnotic gaze and a mouth that was pure magic, sure.

Cady finished the last of her sweet roll and licked her fingers. "You know, I should probably get going. I'll drop one of these off with Dad on my way out." She kissed her mother on the cheek. "I'll see you later."

He'd said he'd give her time, Damon thought as he strode through the farmers' market. God help him, he'd promised it.

And he hadn't gotten a decent night's sleep since.

Over a week had passed, a week during which he hadn't seen her or spoken to her. The time should've gone by in a snap. After all, he was working more than sixteen hours a day. Somehow, though, that still left time to miss her.

It was ironic. He'd been with beautiful women, women who knew every trick in the book, women who'd turned seduction into a vocation. And yet it was thoughts of Cady, her scent, the feel of her breath on his skin, that sent need grinding through him. The other women had come to him freely, and often. Yet Cady was the one he waited for.

"What's with the sour face?"

Damon glanced up to find himself before a table of tomatoes, and Pete Tebeau grinning at him. "Hey, Pete. Nothing's up, just thinking."

"I'd hate to be the person you're thinking about."

If you only knew, my man. "You got my ramps?"

The last of the season, more than likely. After Damon's first buy, Gus had turned into an enthusiastic supplier, boxing them for Pete to sell, not just to the Sextant, but to half the chefs in Portland. The restaurant community didn't know what it owed him, Damon thought sardonically.

"Oh, I almost forgot," Pete said, "the wife keeps asking me to get your recipe for the lobster salad from when we were at your place. She can't stop talking about it."

"Sure. It's easy, as long as you've got fresh lobsters."

Pete grinned. "You kidding? This is Maine. They show up at the caucuses."

"How about some paper?"

Pete dug around by his cash box and unearthed a sheet.

"How was your anniversary?" Damon asked, calculating quantities in his head and writing swiftly. "Was your wife surprised?"

"Overwhelmed, more like. I didn't recognize half of what you fed us but it's the best food I've ever eaten. She hasn't stopped talking about it since." He squinted. "My mom always said that the best way to a man's heart was through his stomach, but I'm starting to wonder if it doesn't work the other way, too. Maybe I should learn how to cook."

And all Damon could think about was the look on Cady's face when he'd put the *croustillant* in her mouth. Absolute pleasure, no reservations.

The way he wanted her to feel when he touched her.

"If you've made it to your twenty-fifth anniversary, I think you've probably already taken care of the heart part, my man," he said aloud, and handed Pete the sheet. "Here's the recipe. And if you decide you want to learn how to cook her something yourself, just ask."

The burly vendor winked. "How about one of them aphrodisiacs? Could you give me a recipe for one of them?"

Damon snorted. "Yeah, sure, I'll get right back to you on that one."

It was too bad aphrodisiacs were just a myth, he thought as he drove down I-95 toward Grace Harbor. Then again, if he tried to feed Cady oysters, he was pretty confident she would run screaming the other way, which was a little bit counter to the desired outcome. Of course, it wasn't about aphrodisiacs anyway. If he wanted to seduce her, he had no doubt she'd be seduced. He could see it in her eyes, feel it in the way she trembled against him. But what would they have then? Only regrets, on both sides.

He needed her to come to him willingly. He needed her trust. He knew he'd changed, he knew he was different than he'd been a decade, or even a few years, before. But somehow, he needed her to believe it.

"I don't know what to think about you," she'd said. In some strange way it was as though, if he could convince her, it would be proof that the change was real.

He pulled in through the trees at the Compass Rose and parked behind the restaurant to unload. Lettuce, ramps, fiddleheads, some hothouse tomatoes and herbs. Roman would arrive soon and they'd get to work, Damon thought as he carried produce boxes inside. Now that the menu was completely converted, there was plenty to do.

And it was making a difference. Business was picking up. He'd made a few calls, put out a quiet word to the food writers he knew. Now, all he could do was sit back, make the best food he knew how to make and wait.

It was becoming a theme in his life.

Then he heard the knock on the door, and turned to see Cady stepping inside, a tray of greens in her hands.

And the waiting stopped.

"Hey."

He turned to welcome her with a smile. In his eyes she read surprise, pleasure and something else that sent one of those little pulses of electricity through her. If she could just get him to stop smiling at her that way, Cady thought, she might have an easier time of it. Certainly she'd have an easier time keeping it together, as opposed to melting into a little puddle on the floor.

But she couldn't keep her mouth from curving in response. It felt too good to see him.

"What have you got there?" He walked closer to see.

"Something you might be interested in." She set the tray on the counter. "Microgreens. At least, I think they still qualify as micro. You tell me."

He wasn't looking at the tray, though. Instead, he was staring at her in dawning delight. "Microgreens? You grew microgreens for me?"

Her face warmed. "Yeah, well, I figured you probably wouldn't find time in between all of your vegetable chopping. I found some stuff about it online and ordered the seeds."

Before she knew what he intended, he pulled her close and gave her a smacking kiss, then lingered a bit longer to do a more thorough job. When he released her, her head was spinning. "Hey," she said.

"I can't believe you did this."

She would get her equilibrium back, Cady told herself. It would just take a few minutes. "I did it for the restaurant," she told him. "I mean, who knows how you would have done? You're a cook, not a gardener."

"You might be surprised," he said. "Wait till you see the kitchen garden I'm putting in."

"Here?"

He laughed. "I've got more respect for my health and safety than to try to plant something on your turf. No, out at the house I'm renting. The backyard's huge. I figure I can put in some squash and tomatoes, corn, maybe a couple of pumpkins for fall."

Pumpkins for fall. He said the words casually but they reverberated in her head. "You're putting in a garden," she repeated.

"This weekend. I already hit the nursery out by the highway to load up."

He was serious, she realized. He was planting something that wouldn't come to fruition for months. Pumpkins for fall. This wasn't the activity of a man who expected to disappear in a few weeks when his ship came in.

This might, just might, be a guy who planned to stick around for a while.

Her wide smile was completely involuntary. "Have you got everything you need?"

"I popped for some tools and a wheelbarrow."

"I mean for the actual garden."

"It's dirt, water and seeds, right? And maybe some fertilizer?"

She rolled her eyes. "Sure, just like bread is water and flour. You've got to make sure the soil's fertile. If it's just been fallow, you're going to need manure or compost to enrich it."

"What do you mean, enrich it? It's dirt, not a pan sauce. The weeds are doing fine without my help."

"That's why they're weeds. If you want to grow good vegetables, especially up here, you need the right kind of soil."

He sighed. "Okay, maybe you'd better make me a list. Or you could just come tutor me." He flicked her a glance of amusement.

"All right." The words took both of them by surprise. She hadn't planned to agree, hadn't planned to help. And yet…

Pumpkins for fall.

Pumpkins for fall, and perhaps a very different man than she'd first judged him to be.

"You're going to come help?" he asked. "You mean it?"

Nervous tension bubbled through her. It was only an offer to do yard work, Cady told herself, but she knew different.

And so did he.

"For the afternoon," she qualified hastily, "just to get you started. I can't do it tomorrow, though, because I'm going to Portland to see my sister. Anyway, there's still a risk of frost. You'd be better off waiting another week."

"How about next Sunday?"

She nodded. "I'll bring some tools and a wheelbarrow. And a load of manure."

"Thanks… I think," he added after a beat. "Tell you what.

I'll make you a deal—you help me put in the garden and I'll cook you dinner."

She gave him a suspicious look. "This isn't part of your 'educate my palate' program, is it? Are you going to cook me something weird like squid brains?"

"Squid brains," he repeated thoughtfully. "Now, that's an intriguing—"

"Forget it," she cut him off.

"Ah hell, you never let me have any fun. Okay, fine, you help with the garden, I'll cook you a non-squid-brain dinner. Sound like a plan?"

What it sounded like was a date. She took an unsteady breath. "It's your weekend. Are you sure you want to cook?"

"Are you sure you want to garden?"

It was an out, she recognized, but she didn't take it. She'd spent the week thinking about him, about them, and she hadn't come up with any answers. In agreeing to help, though, she realized that she'd known all along what she wanted to do. "Yeah," she said. "You helped us move the furniture. This is payback. Anyway, it'll keep me out of trouble."

"Are you sure of that?" He studied her.

"What, you don't think I can take you down?" she said lightly.

"Be my guest." It wasn't said in the tone of a school yard taunt. He meant it.

She flushed.

"Okay, we're on for Sunday," he said, letting her off the hook. "I can get you directions later in the week."

"Good." She nodded and turned to leave, but he caught her wrist to stop her.

Cady froze. "I should go."

"I never really thanked you for the microgreens," he said softly.

Her heart began to thump harder. "Oh. Well. It's not a big

deal. It was to help out the restaurant…or my parents." It was hard to think when the heat from his fingers was spreading up her arm.

"I'd like to think you did it for me," he murmured and trapped her hands between his own. "Your fingers are freezing."

"It's cold out."

Not inside, though, not here where his palms and fingers were mesmerizingly warm against her skin. Not soft—a man with his job would never have soft hands—but they were strong, capable and somehow soothing. The ropes of sinew and muscle in his forearms spoke of power and yet his hold on her was gentle.

And if she stayed here with his hands wrapped around hers much longer, she might never leave. "I should go," she said, making herself pull away from him. "I have work."

"All right." Those dark eyes with their flecks of gold gazed steadily at her. "Next Sunday is a long time away."

"I think you'll survive."

"You know, there's a restaurant supply store up in Portland I keep meaning to get to. I need an immersion circulator."

"An immersion what?"

"An immersion circulator. To do *sous vide*. Never mind," he said, mouth curving in amusement. "The thing is, maybe we could carpool."

"To Portland?"

"That's the idea."

It was simultaneously appealing and alarming. "I'm going to be there most of the day," she said doubtfully.

"I'm sure I can find things to do. Give me a chance to look around the city. Tell you what. We can even take my car."

"You only say that because you're afraid of my driving."

He patted her shoulder. "Make that terrified, Mario Andretti, terrified."

Chapter Ten

"Are you sure we're related?" Cady threw a suspicious glance at her older sister, Max. Her gorgeous sister, Max, her statuesque sister, Max, her sophisticated sister, Max—only three of the many ways they differed.

The fourth sat before them.

"For heaven's sakes, I'm not trying to lop off a limb, Cady," Max said in exasperation. "I just want to go in and look at that dress."

"But that's the sixth place you've stopped," Cady said. It wasn't a whine, not precisely. "And you've already bought something."

"For work. This would be for play." Max admired the fuchsia tank dress in the store window.

"I thought we were just walking back to your place from lunch. I didn't know we were on a shopping trip."

"We *are* walking back to my place. I just believe in multi-tasking."

"Multitasking," Cady grumbled.

"I didn't notice you complaining when we went into the chocolate shop," Max threw over her shoulder as they stepped inside.

The store had smooth maple floors, terrifyingly chic sales-clerks and pricey-looking clothes. Then again, down in the heart of Portland's Old Port district, where Max lived, most of the boutiques were pricey.

"We're still going to find time to talk about the party, right?" Cady asked.

Max stuck her head over the top of the dressing room door. "Of course we're going to." With a snap, she opened the catch of the door and stepped out.

"You know, if you weren't my sister, I'd have to hate you." Cady watched her turn to and fro before the mirror.

"And if you weren't my sister, I'd have to hate you," Max rejoined.

Cady blinked. "Why?"

"Oh, being your own boss with no office bs, wearing jeans to work every day, having that gorgeous red hair." Max waved away the hovering salesclerk and turned to the dressing room with a satisfied nod.

"You wouldn't say that if you had skin that blushed every ten minutes."

Max peeked over the top of the door again. "What have you been up to that you're blushing about?"

"Oh, well, you know," Cady said awkwardly.

"I don't." Max stepped back out. "But it sounds like I should. Come on, let's pay for this and go back home so I can feed you wine and pump you for details."

Out on the street, the breeze off the water was mild enough to enjoy without a jacket. "Mmm, I love the first really warm day of the year," Max said. "It makes you believe summer's really going to happen."

"You must believe in it, considering how much you spent on that dress."

"I'll get a lot of wear out of that dress." The sun was warm on their shoulders as they walked over the cobblestones. "Back to this blushing thing, what's the deal?"

"Nothing. Not much, anyway," Cady amended.

"Not much? What, are you moonlighting at a strip club? Is there a twenty-four-hour Cady Cam on the Internet?" Max looked at her more closely. "Or do you have a new guy?"

And Cady felt the telltale flush spread up her cheeks.

"Oh, perfect, new guy," Max said gleefully as they turned into the doorway that led to her loft. "I'm definitely feeding you wine now."

Sunlight streaming through the skylights made parallelograms on the exposed-brick walls of the loft. Cady wandered around, looking at the sepia-toned photographs of old diners Max had hung on the walls. Amy Winehouse played in the background.

"Tell me about your guy," Max called over from the kitchen, her voice muffled as she reached into a cabinet for wineglasses. "Who is he, where did you meet, what's he like?"

Cady flopped on the squashy leather sofa. "Is this true/false or multiple choice?"

"Essay." Max opened the bottle.

"First of all, he's not my guy."

"Have you gone out?"

"No," Cady said, but she made the strategic error of looking down.

Max's eyes brightened. "Kissed?"

"Once or twice," she acknowledged grudgingly.

"Well, which is it? Once or twice?"

"Twice, I guess."

"You're not sure?"

Cady thought back to the feel of Damon's mouth over hers. "Oh yeah, I'm sure."

"Well, kissing counts in my book," Max said briskly, handing Cady her wine and settling on the sofa. She raised her glass. "To things that count."

"Things that count," Cady echoed.

"And your guy." Max settled on the couch facing Cady and crossed her legs. "So?"

"So?"

"So, dish. What's he like?"

Cady gave in, drawing her legs up before her on the couch. "Oh, funny, smart, charming. Confident. He just assumes everything's going to go his way and it does."

"Not a G-boy, is he?"

"Hardly. More like a bad boy. He doesn't seem to pay a lot of attention to rules," she continued, not noticing the sharp glance her sister gave her. "But he busts his behind to do what he thinks needs to get done."

"Ah, the old charming renegade type. That can be sexy. Dangerous, but sexy."

"He is, too much for his own good."

"But you've managed to resist him so far?"

"Yeah."

"It's a good lesson for him." Max took a swallow of wine. "A man should never underestimate a McBain woman."

"Oh, I think he's figured out the stubborn Scot part already." Cady laughed.

"Good for him. It'll come as less of a shock, getting used to it now. And what do we call him?" At Cady's hesitation, she frowned. "What? Tell me."

"You can't breathe a word to Mom and Dad."

Max gave her a suspicious stare. "Why do I not get a good feeling about this? Who is he?"

Cady cleared her throat. "Um, Damon Hurst."

"Damon Hurst?" She stared. "You mean the new chef? *That* Damon Hurst?"

"Do you know of another one?"

"No, but I was sort of hoping that you did. You know, Mom told me you were ranting about him like he was the devil incarnate when he first showed up, but you've been here four hours and you haven't made a peep. I was kind of wondering." She shook her head as though she was a wet dog. "Cady, why in God's name are you getting involved with a guy like Damon Hurst?"

"Why shouldn't I? Because I'm not some celebrity babe?" Cady retorted.

"No. Because you're…" Inexperienced, Max thought, and more vulnerable than anyone would guess from the prickly attitude. She let out a breath. "You're my kid sister, okay? I don't want some get-around guy getting around with you."

"I'm twenty-seven, Max, and he's not going to. Give me some credit. I mean, we're not really even involved yet."

"Except for the kissing part."

"Except for the kissing part," Cady admitted.

"That's a pretty big part."

Cady rested her chin on her knees. "I know it doesn't make sense, but something happens when I get around him. I mean, I can sit here talking to you and I know I'm nuts. I'm not his type. He's out of my league and I should just get the hell away. But when I'm with him, when he looks at me—" she shook her head "—none of that matters. It all goes away and I just believe him. So what do I do, go with my head or go with my gut? You know about guys, Max. What do I do?"

"Does he make you feel good?"

"Make me feel good?" Cady repeated. And slowly a smile bloomed across her face. "Incredible, more like. It's the way I always thought it was supposed to be. Like it happens for everybody else. I mean, you know how it's been with me. I'm interested in a guy and he doesn't know I exist, or if he does, he runs the other way. Damon makes me feel special, like I matter. It feels like…"

"Like what?"

"Oh, this'll sound goofy but remember this afternoon when we were in that cold store and then we stepped back out on the street and into the sunlight? It feels like that. Warm and…and golden." She rolled her eyes. "Does it sound as bad as I think it does?"

"It sounds nice." And if this joker was messing with her, Max would cheerfully see him talking soprano. Max took a breath. "Are you going to sleep with him?"

There was a long silence. "Yeah," Cady said softly, "I'm going to. Part of me thinks I'm out of my mind to take the risk, but the other part thinks I'd be out of my mind to pass it up. I mean, you know my record. I may never come across another guy who'll give me the time of day, let alone luck out with a guy like him."

"You ask me, he's the one who's lucky," Max said.

"You say that because you're biased."

"No, I say that because I'm your big sister and I know best."

"Always pulling rank," Cady groused. "I swear, if I—" The sound of a cell phone ring tone cut her off. "Just a sec, let me get this. It might be Damon." She walked over to her jacket and fished the handset out of her pocket. "Hello? Oh, hi."

The words were breathless, the smile wide.

Max watched from across the room. The swaths of sunlight on the wall had faded as day moved into afternoon, but as she watched, she saw Cady glow, saw the pleasure and hope in her eyes.

Saw what Cady hadn't yet admitted to herself.

Max rose and carried the wineglasses back to the kitchen. "What's the deal?" she asked as Cady put her hand over the phone.

"He wants to know if I have any idea when I want to leave," Cady said.

"Well, it's about four. We still need to talk about Dad's party for a while. Tell him to meet us at Soleil on Exchange Street at five-thirty. We'll go to dinner."

"Dinner?" Cady squeaked.

"Dinner," Max said firmly. "I want to check this guy out."

Cady saw him as they turned the corner to Soleil, a little bistro tucked away in one of the old brick buildings down in the Old Port. He leaned against the wall by the door in his leather jacket, looking relaxed, dark and just a bit reckless. Then again, she felt just a bit reckless herself.

For a few steps, she watched him, admiring that gorgeous face, that long, lean body. Definitely out of her league, but she was going to go with it until whoever it was that pulled the levers in the universe realized there'd been a mistake and changed everything back.

And then he turned and their gazes locked and it was like the thump of power from an electrical shock jolting through her. Connection, more intense than it had ever been. Every step felt weighted with importance, every instant felt crystalline and shimmering.

"I guess you found it." Her voice came out oddly breathless as they stopped before him.

"I guess I did," he agreed.

"You could have gone inside."

"I wanted to wait for you. Besides, I'm inside too much as it is. It's nice to see the sun for a change. It's nice to see you, too," he added.

"Oh. Well." She sounded like an idiot, Cady thought.

"I take it this is your sister?" He turned to Max. "Nice to meet you. I'm Damon Hurst."

"I'm Max McBain," she said, shaking his hand. "I'm also hungry."

Damon grinned. "Then I guess we should go inside."

The restaurant was narrow, the exposed brick walls hung with mirrors to make the space seem bigger than it was. Industrial heater vents trailed over the ceiling high above them. Pendant lamps in blue and red and green hung down low. In the open kitchen tucked in the back corner, the sounds of sizzling rose as white-capped chefs did magical things with fish and fowl, sending out scents that had Cady's mouth watering.

"How was your trip to the restaurant supply store?" Cady asked as the waitress opened the wine. "Did you get your immersion circulator?"

"I did. We'll be using it to make some of the food for your father's party."

"Ah, you're the chef for that," Max said.

"The assistant," he corrected. "Roman, the sous chef, had a lot of the groundwork done already when I got here, and Cady can tell you, he's a pretty good cook himself. I'm not going to come in and take over. I'm just pitching in where he asks me to."

It was like him, Cady realized. For all that she'd heard about his ego, she'd never once seen it in evidence while he'd been at the Sextant.

"What are you guys making?" Max asked.

"Oh, lobster, pork chops with rosemary cider sauce, duck breast with blueberry coulis. Sorry—" his eyes glimmered at Cady "—no pizza. Although we did consider having cheese Danish for dessert."

Max was used to being looked at by men. She was accustomed to capturing their full attention, whether she wanted it or not. As appetizers gave way to entrées, and on to dessert, she didn't see what she'd feared. Oh, Damon was good company. He joked, made clever comments, asked all the right questions, but with every moment that passed, one thing was clear.

He had eyes only for Cady.

As for Max, he might as well have been talking to their brother, Walker. He was merely polite to their waitress, who was no slouch herself in the looks department.

And when Cady rose to go to the ladies' room, he turned to watch her go.

Max's smile widened. "What's it like for you as a chef, going out to dinner? Is it a busman's holiday?"

Damon glanced back over at her. "Even busmen have to eat."

"So you're not thinking about the food?"

"Oh, I'm always thinking about the food, no matter where I am, the same way Cady probably notices the plants. If I'm in a restaurant, I'm interested in their ingredients, I'm interested in their influences."

"Do you ever take recipes back to your own place?"

"That's like one artist trying to paint like another. I always want to take it in a different direction, even if I like the flavors. I thought their duck was good but I'd probably experiment around with adding some roasted poblano to the tomato coulis, get a hotter counterpoint to the sweet."

"A hot tomato sauce?"

"Maybe. The idea is I do my own riff on it. Whatever I come up with won't be a copy, it'll be my interpretation." He took a swallow of wine. "Then again, that's really what cooking's all about anyway. Like Marco Pierre White said, there's nothing new under the sun, we're all just refining what came before."

"And is that what you're doing here? Refining what came before?"

He leaned back and studied her. "Why do I get the idea we're not talking about food anymore?"

"Interesting that you'd put that interpretation on it."

Humor hovered at the corners of his mouth. "Is this the part where you start cracking your knuckles and telling me I better not mess with your sister?"

"I'd hope you know enough about my sister by now to know that she's perfectly capable of cracking her own knuckles. I'll just say she deserves you to be straight and she deserves the best you can give her."

"I know enough about her by now to be sure of that, too."

"Well, then—" Max tipped her head "—it appears we're in agreement."

Across the room, Cady approached.

"What are you two looking so serious about?" she asked, sliding into her chair.

Max locked eyes with Damon and smiled. "Hot tomatoes," she said. "We're talking about hot tomatoes."

Chapter Eleven

"God, I love this time of year," Cady said, stretching in the front seat of Damon's car as they headed south from Portland toward Grace Harbor.

He glanced over and watched her just a beat too long. "Why's that?"

"Oh, the sun's out. The days last forever. You know summer's coming but the mobs haven't descended yet. The town still belongs to us." The slanting rays of the setting sun felt warm on her skin.

"The mobs?"

"The summer people. You'll see. How long does it take you to get into town from where you live?"

Damon moved his head. "I don't know, fifteen, twenty minutes?"

"Plan for an hour when the season hits."

"When's that?"

"Fourth of July weekend, usually."

"Not in June?" He changed lanes to pass a truck.

"Not warm enough yet," she said. "But when July hits it's something else. Grace Harbor turns into a whole different place when the out-of-towners show up."

"You're not big on out-of-towners, I take it." His glance this time was sidelong, his eyes dark in the deepening dusk.

And she felt the little whisper of arousal. "That depends on the out-of-towner," she said.

"Good to know." He paused. "Why live in Grace Harbor, then? If it gets so crowded, why not go somewhere else?"

"Because it's home," she said simply. "Because, oh, I don't know, because of the way the water looks in the morning when the sun comes up. Because of the way the air smells after it snows. Because I can look at the rhododendrons by the back porch and remember planting them with my dad when I was in third grade."

He didn't answer right away. "Sounds nice," he said finally.

And was it her imagination or did she hear the faintest whisper of wistfulness in his voice? "So, where did you grow up?" She kept her voice casual.

"Pretty much everywhere. I was an Air Force brat," he elaborated. "We'd lived in five states and two countries by the time I was ten."

"Did you like moving around?"

"Would you?" He smiled humorlessly. "Ah, it wasn't so bad while my mom was alive."

While his mom was alive. "When did you lose her?"

"When I was twelve. Cancer," he said in answer to her unspoken question. "She went pretty fast."

Cady couldn't imagine it. "I'm sorry," she said softly and reached out to squeeze his hand.

"Thanks. It was a long time ago."

"But you still miss her."

"Yeah, I do." His fingers tangled with hers. "You're lucky to have your folks."

"I know. But you have your dad, at least. So he was in the Air Force?"

"Still is, I guess." Damon reached over to flick on the heat.

"You guess?" she asked.

"We haven't talked in a while."

"How long is a while?"

"How about not this century?"

She stared. "You haven't talked to your father in eight years?" A people person she might not be, but it was impossible to imagine not talking to family.

Damon smiled faintly. "We're not what you would call close."

"Why's that?"

"Let's just say we had different ideas on who I should be. He wanted a private, not a son. The funny thing is, I probably wouldn't have wound up being a chef if it weren't for him."

"He taught you to cook?"

"In a manner of speaking. I started trying to mess around in the kitchen after my mother died, mostly out of self-defense. It was either that or eat what my dad came up with, or MREs when he didn't want to deal with it."

"MREs?"

"Meals ready to eat. What they feed troops in the field."

Twelve years old, she thought, no mother, a father who clearly didn't give a damn. It squeezed her heart.

"Couldn't you stay with relatives?"

"Her parents came from Yankee money, thought she'd married beneath her. My father figured we ought to be able to solve our own problems. And I wasn't what you'd call a tractable kid."

It had gotten full dark. The taillights of the cars ahead shone red. "How did you make the leap from home to a restaurant kitchen?" Cady asked. "Culinary school?"

"Kind of by accident, like a lot of cooks, I think. We were stationed in West Germany. I was about sixteen and I'd gotten into a…scrap, you might say. The colonel—"

"The colonel?"

"My father. He decided I needed to do something productive with my time, get a job. So I went to a local restaurant and convinced the chef to take me on. I basically chopped carrots, turned potatoes for a few hours after school."

"I'm guessing that wasn't exactly what your father had in mind."

"Not exactly. On the other hand, I was under supervision and bringing home dinner. After a while, he got used to it. The funny thing was, a lot of what helped me survive in that kitchen I'd learned from him."

"How to open MREs?"

He grinned. "How to tune out the flack and get the job done. The chef was from Alsace, just over the border. Maybe he was insulted that he had to cook in Germany, I don't know. He was sure happy to thumb his nose at the German government and fake the papers I needed to work. The minute he got into the kitchen, though, he was an absolute madman. All the other prep cooks were terrified. If you didn't chop the shallots or celery or the carrots to the exact millimeter, he'd throw it all across the room. Then you'd have to clean up and chop more of them to his standards *and* work extra hours because you'd been responsible for wasting food."

"Sounds like a heck of a guy."

Damon moved his shoulders. "He was just trying to teach us discipline. I only figured that part out later. It's not so easy when you're dealing with a pack of newbies like he was. Sometimes you just have to instill fear." His mouth curved.

"Is that what you were doing when you yelled at your chefs on TV?"

"Sometimes. Everybody wants to be a star. Some of them

had a tendency to showboat and screw things up." The corners of his eyes crinkled. "Sometimes, we'd planned it in advance just for the drama. I already had the rep from Pommes de Terre. I figured I had to live up to it."

"So to speak," she said.

"So to speak. Besides, there's something about a restaurant kitchen that brings out the crazy side of people. I don't know if it's the hours, or the pressure, or the workload, but it turns even reasonable people into screamers."

"Now I know why I didn't get to you back at the beginning."

He turned to look at her and there was heat in his gaze. "Oh, you got to me, all right."

And a slow tug of wanting began down low in her belly. They were driving down the open highway, Cady reminded herself. It took her two tries to speak. "So." She licked her lips. "You were working for the screamer. What happened then?"

"You want more?"

She wanted everything.

"Well," he continued, "I worked at the restaurant for a year and a half, every day after school. After a while, I learned. By the time I left, he'd made me weekend sous chef."

"Not bad for a kid who was, what, seventeen?"

He nodded. "The day I turned eighteen, he sat me down in the dining room between lunch and dinner service and poured me a glass of claret. Told me he had a friend in Provence, a chef who would let me work in his kitchen. More important, the friend had contacts in half of the Michelin-starred restaurants in France. If I wanted to be a chef, all I had to do was ask."

"What did your father say?"

Damon shrugged. "What could he say? I was over age, he couldn't stop me." He flicked on his blinker and got over to the right. They were at the Grace Harbor exit, Cady realized.

"I left and spent two and a half years working my way

across France," Damon went on, "learning everything I could. Then in Lyon, I lucked out and got a chance to work in Paul Descour's kitchen. When he moved to New York to open a restaurant, I went with him."

"And the rest is history," she said lightly.

"History," he reflected. "That makes it sound more important than it is."

"It is important. The past is what makes you who you are."

"I'm less interested in the past than I am in what happens next." He pulled off onto the exit ramp. "The past might make you who you are, but it's who you are that decides where you go."

The car slowed and came to a stop, the roar of highway noise gradually fading away to the barely audible hum of the idling engine. A red light hung ahead of them in the darkness. Cady swallowed. "And where do you want to go?"

"Right now, somewhere quiet and alone with you."

His words seemed to echo in the silence of the car. She could hear each separate beat of her heart. She knew that the choice was still hers, she had only to make it. And in making it, she would sever herself irreversibly from all that had come before.

She took a breath. "The light's green," she said.

Knowing that she wanted to do something and actually doing it were two very different things, Cady realized as they climbed the steps to the dark porch of her rental duplex. During the drive from the highway, the nerves had come back. Her fingers were clumsy as she fumbled with her keys.

The problem was that she didn't know what to do. She didn't know how to be with him. Above all things, she desperately wanted the sex to be good. She couldn't bear for it to turn into a disappointment.

For either of them.

"No lights?" he asked, making her jump.

"I didn't turn any on before I left. I thought I'd be coming home in daylight."

"You could have somebody in here rifling the place." He stepped in close behind her. "Good thing I'm here."

"That's right," she said. "You could whisk them to death."

"Careful," he murmured in her ear. "You don't want to underestimate me."

It wasn't possible, she thought as she opened the door and stepped inside. And as she flipped on the lights, she was more aware of her every move than she ever had been before.

A generous person might have called her duplex compact. The furniture was well-worn, basic, although early-American garage sale might have been a more accurate description. The disorder was greater than it might have been if she'd had warning, but not much. It suited her just fine. Seeing it through Damon's eyes, though, made her self-conscious.

Then again, she felt awkward in general. They both knew why they were there, they both knew what they wanted, and yet there was this breathless wait, this unaccountable distance. And he was making no move to bridge the gap.

Her stomach tightened. "You want something to drink?"

"Sure."

Desperate to break the tension, Cady walked into her galley-style kitchen. "Not wine, I don't have any."

"That's all right." He followed her.

"I have Coke." She opened the refrigerator. "And, uh, well, Coke."

He pressed his lips to the back of her neck and she jolted. "And, uh, water…"

He journeyed up to nibble her earlobe.

"And…"

"I don't care about drinking." He turned her to face him, closing the refrigerator door.

"What do you want—"

"You, right now," he said, and pulled her to him.

In the midst of all the uncertainty, there was this between them, this connection, this immediacy, this thing that took her outside herself and made her a part of him, a part of what they made together. She'd worried about it all turning sour the way her other experiences had, but no kiss had ever carried her along like this.

And all of her self-consciousness melted away in the heat of his mouth. For it was impossible to be self-conscious when every fiber of her was busy being aware, busy feeling the press of his lips, the slick tease of his tongue, the delicious stroke of his hands down her body. He nibbled at her lips as though she were some exotic delicacy, inhaled her scent the way she'd seen him savor the aroma of a ripe pear at the market.

He pushed her jacket off her shoulders and let it drop to the floor, kept his mouth fused to hers as he shucked off his own. And then he pulled her to him, fit them together and she'd never imagined anything could feel so glorious.

Deep within her, something began to grow, some tension, some awareness, some deep-seated need. This time, when he broke the kiss, she dragged his head back down to hers. This time, she was the one who demanded, she was the one who teased, she was the one who took.

Damon felt the wanting drum in his veins. He walked her backward so that she was against the wall, catching her hands and pressing them against the wallpaper on either side of her head and devoting all his concentration to the kiss.

Because it was a kiss worth concentrating on.

The other times had been stolen moments, distracting, if all the more exciting, because of the chance of discovery. This, though, this was just about the two of them. There would be no interruptions, there would be no diversions. This time, this place was just for them, and for just this night they had all the time in the world.

He worked his way across her cheek, smoother than he'd have ever guessed. "You smell like apples," he muttered against the skin of her throat. "Why do you always smell like apples?"

"Shampoo," she said breathlessly.

Of course it would be something like shampoo and not cologne. It was one of the delightful mysteries of her, that she drove him nuts without ever once trying. And that she had no idea she was doing it.

"It makes me want to take a bite of you," he said softly. He nipped at her and heard the catch of her breath.

And there was this, the artless way she responded to the least thing he did. He'd been with women who were wildcats in bed. It had excited him in passing, perhaps, but it always left him with the uneasy feeling that it was a performance, for them and for him. With Cady, he knew her reactions were real. Because she was real. He could feel her trembling, feel the quick jolt of surprise as he licked his way down the smooth skin over her collarbone, and lower, into the shallow vee between her breasts.

Cady moaned at the heat of his breath against her skin, at the warmth of his mouth as he did things to her, divine things, even as his nimble fingers ran down the buttons of her shirt, clearing the way. When he pulled her shirt open and slid it off her shoulders, there was no room for self-consciousness. In the breathless rush of the moment, all she could think of was the touch of his hands, the taste of his mouth, the hard-muscled body under her fingers.

The steps to the bedroom were few; there was no need to separate to reach it. When they stumbled over the threshold, they stumbled together, and when they fell to the bed, they fell as one.

It was a race, now. He unbuttoned her jeans and she moved to help him strip them off. Then he tore off his own clothing, flinging it aside impatiently. There was no time, there was no patience, there was only need, need driving them both.

Then they were body to body, skin to skin, all heat and texture and an overwhelming rush of sensation that swept through her like the wind of a nor'easter.

There would be time, Damon thought feverishly. There would be time to pleasure her with mouth and hands, but right now he had to be in her, to feel her clench around him, to take her up until she'd reached the point where she couldn't hold back, watch her tumble over into ecstasy.

And know he was the one who'd taken her there.

Her hands urged him on, her mouth seduced. When he moved to poise himself over her body, she stared up at him, her eyes darkened to green, her lips parted on a gasp. Then he shifted and drove into her. And the cry she gave nearly put him over the edge.

Her fingers pressed against the slick muscles of his back, feeling them surge and tighten with each stroke. And the rhythm, the rhythm caught her up until she was driving to meet him, wrapping her legs around his waist so that she could go with him, their bodies moving in a kind of contrapuntal rhythm of pleasure.

And, oh, it was almost more than she could stand, the feel of him inside her, on her, around her, against her, driving her, into her, and taking her, taking her, taking her. And suddenly, it was like the start of a roller-coaster ride. One moment, the tension was winding tighter and tighter until she swore she couldn't bear it, and then suddenly, shockingly, she was flying over some invisible edge she'd never dreamed of, the pleasure exploding through her body out to her fingertips so that she was crying out, shaking against him, even as he groaned and spilled himself.

And in a moment, in an instant, in an eternity, Cady McBain finally understood what all the fuss was about.

* * *

"Good Lord." Cady half laughed. She wanted to run, she wanted to leap, she wanted to shout out to the skies. She'd just been through the most incredible experience of her entire life. Nothing that had gone before had prepared her for it. And now that she knew, nothing would be the same.

Damon rolled over onto his back.

"Are you all right?"

"Trying to remember how to breathe," he said. "I'll get it in a minute."

"So that's what sex is like in the big city."

He gave a low laugh. "Uh, well, not exactly."

Not exactly? How, not exactly? Cady wondered. She couldn't tell from his tone. She'd thought that it had been good for both of them, but maybe he was used to something else. So what if he'd rocked her world? Maybe she'd merely gotten him off, no more, no less. Nerves suddenly seized her. Feeling exposed, she moved to rise.

"Where are you going?"

"I'm just—"

He looped an arm around her and pulled her on top of him. "What's wrong?"

"Nothing." She tried to squirm away but found herself held tight. "I just… I'm sorry it wasn't what you're used to."

"What do you mean? Were you here in the room with me two minutes ago?"

"I haven't done this a whole lot, okay?" she said defensively. "Maybe I don't keep up with your Manhattan girlfriends. I don't know any of those tricks with feather dusters and hair scrunchies and spearmint toothpaste."

He gave her a perplexed look. "Hair scrunchies?"

"Hair bands. You put them around…" She waved toward his crotch and flushed. "My girlfriend Tania reads a lot."

"I guess so. Well, in case you didn't notice, we did just fine without the spearmint toothpaste and if you come at me with a hair scrunchie, I'm going to run." He pressed a kiss on her. "Look, I'm not big on comparing, but I've never been through anything quite like that before. And I mean that in a good way."

"Oh. Well, then." She relaxed infinitesimally.

"And you don't have to tell me anything but it sounds like maybe you've been with some idiots who were too stupid to appreciate you...and maybe too clumsy or clueless to give you any reason to appreciate them. You're amazing. What just happened was amazing."

"Really?"

"Trust me." His gaze was steady on hers. "And if you don't believe me, I'll be happy to demonstrate it again."

"Well, I might need some convincing," she said, pressing her mouth to his.

"Coming right up, ma'am."

"Oh, I hope so," she breathed.

Chapter Twelve

Damon stood at the stove in the Sextant kitchen, whistling to himself. He'd been doing that a lot the past few days.

It was strange to feel so good. For years, he'd gone to the parties and bars to look for it. He hadn't found it; instead, what mattered to him most had slipped away. Grace Harbor didn't have the nightlife he'd grown accustomed to but oddly enough, he didn't miss it a lick. He felt good at work, he felt good at home, and especially he felt good with Cady.

She fit his life in a way he couldn't explain. She wasn't easy. She might have challenged him but she seldom bored him. She amused him, kept him guessing.

Most of all, she excited him.

And it wasn't just her. He'd found his kitchen mojo again. He was back at the stove, back in the one place he'd ever truly belonged. He was doing what he loved. And he was with a woman he—

Wanted to be with. He completed the thought hastily and turned back to the stove to splash a bit of port into the cider sauce he was working on.

Mornings, when the sun had just come up, were the part of the day he liked best. The rest of the staff hadn't arrived. It was just him, maybe with Roman working quietly at the far end of the kitchen. The unstructured time gave him a chance to experiment, a chance to refine the new cuisine he was gradually developing.

He tasted the sauce, letting the flavors roll over his tongue, letting the profile build. Then he began to analyze it. Was there enough acidity to bring out the sweetness? Did the complexity added by shallots and herbs enhance the flavor or mask it?

Thoughtfully, he added a squeeze of lemon juice, a dash of cider vinegar and tried it again. Leaning down to sniff it, he inhaled the scent of apples.

And he wasn't thinking about cider sauce anymore. He was remembering Cady, skin rosy by lamplight as she rode him, finding her own pleasure, her face transforming as she shivered over into climax, quaking against him, clenching around him—

"Do you realize what you've done?" Amanda McBain burst into the kitchen, Ian hot on her heels.

"What?" Damon jerked around to stare at them both. Cady? he wondered for a frantic instant before registering the smiles on their faces. Not smiles, he corrected himself, ear-to-ear grins.

"The *Globe*. Don't tell me you haven't seen it." Amanda's eyes were glimmering, excitement coming off her in waves. She brandished the food section of the Boston newspaper, the part that talked about recipes and menu planning and cooking.

And restaurants.

Damon felt the adrenaline start to pump through him. He'd lost track, he realized. Preoccupied with the restaurant and

Cady, he'd forgotten it was Wednesday, the day the paper ran its main restaurant reviews.

And on the front of the section was a picture of the beef tenderloin with truffled fois gras sauce, inset with a photo of the restaurant. Hurst Steers Sextant to Top, trumpeted the headline.

> Damon Hurst is back and his food is exquisite. Don't miss the Sextant if you're visiting the state, and if you're not visiting, make the drive anyway while you can. It's worth it.

"Four stars," Amanda said, hugging him elatedly. "They never give four stars."

"Hell of a job, son." Ian shook his hand and slapped his shoulder.

Roman came over to read along as Damon stared at the print.

> At a time when the prevailing restaurant philosophy is to put as many things on the plate as possible, Hurst understands that less is sometimes more. There is complexity, but the flavors have room to work together. The result is food that intrigues the palate without overwhelming...

In the mix of emotions that swirled within him as he read the review, he felt most of all validation. Find a good restaurant with room to grow and turn it into something, Paul had said, and he'd done just that. He still had the skills that had taken him to the top and he'd shown it. He'd reinvented himself.

He was back.

Next to him, Roman gave a start of surprise. "Hey, Chef, did you see this part? 'If the tenderloin and scallops and lobster are irresistible, the ramp-wrapped shrimp appetizer is a revelation.' A revelation, they say. Ramp-wrapped shrimp," Roman repeated giddily. "That's me."

Damon slapped him on the back, an effervescence building in his blood. "That is you, Roman. Your first mention in a review. How does it feel?"

Roman grinned. "Like we're winners."

And Amanda and Ian looked on, for all the world, like proud parents.

"Okay, we've got something to celebrate here," Ian said. "Make family meal tonight special, whatever you want. And wine. We'll all have a toast."

A family, Damon thought. For the first time in his life, he felt a part of one.

"'This isn't Pommes de Terre at a new address,'" Tania read aloud from the paper as Cady drove them into Grace Harbor. "'Hurst is bringing us something—' Whoa!" Tania stomped her foot on the floorboard.

Cady glanced at her. "What?"

"What?" she demanded. "Do you know you almost took the fender off that Navigator?"

"He moved when the light changed," Cady said reasonably.

Tania made the sign of the cross. "What possessed me to get in a car with you?"

"Your car's in the shop getting a new battery and you needed a ride," Cady reminded her.

"Oh, yeah."

"That means your job is to read the review."

"This is great stuff. Let's see, where was I? Right. 'Hurst is bringing us something entirely new, presenting fresh takes on classic down east ingredients while reinventing New England favorites with a sure hand.' You never told me anything about his sure hands." She gave Cady a sidelong glance.

"You never asked."

"I shouldn't have had to. We did the twin bonding ceremony in third grade, don't you remember? I'm your best friend. You're supposed to tell me everything. Although so far, you haven't told me much."

"Oh, well, you know," Cady said evasively. "You have enough stories for both of us."

"I don't know, with those sure hands involved, he could have come up with something entirely new I should know about. I think you're holding out on me, girlfriend."

"It's for your own good. I'm worried about your tender sensibilities."

In reality, it was her own sensibilities she was worried about. She didn't talk about it because she didn't know how to. And she wasn't sure she wanted to. What was between her and Damon seemed improbable, fantastic, far too fragile to expose to the public eye, even to a friend like Tania.

"The bigger question," Tania went on, "is why haven't I met this god yet?"

"He's busy presenting fresh takes on classic New England ingredients, didn't you read?"

"He can't be that busy," Tania complained.

Cady fought a smile. "You want to meet him, come to the restaurant."

"Oh, like that's going to happen now. You guys are going to be mobbed."

"It's only a review in the Boston paper."

"Haven't you heard of the Internet? Trust me, this is going to get around. Not just Boston. I'm betting you're going to see people coming in from New York and all over. Word's going to get out. Even if he did get kicked off the Cooking Channel, Damon Hurst is a big name."

Cady had grown up with Grace Harbor's split personality, where for the few short weeks of high summer, the friendly, sleepy town she knew became a crowded, chaotic mass of sunburned strangers. She was used to having the place she loved taken over by out-of-towners.

She wasn't at all sure how she felt about a sudden influx of year-round foodies coming for Damon.

"It'll be good for the restaurant," she said aloud as she pulled to a stop in front of Tania's salon. "Good news for my parents. You should've heard my mom when she called this morning. She was so psyched."

"What about your hunka hunka burnin' love?" Tania asked.

"It'll be good for him, too," Cady said. And she believed that. She just wasn't sure it was good for her.

The house was a sand-colored Colonial, built on spec by a contractor who'd lost it to foreclosure when the housing market crashed. He'd planned to build an entire development. So far, Damon's only neighbors were raccoons, wild turkeys and deer.

"The landlord was thrilled when I took it," Damon said. "He told me it had been empty for almost a year."

"I don't see why. It's perfect out here—this whole area all to yourself, no one to bother you."

"No one to help dig you out if you get stuck in the snow," he chimed in.

"Forget snow. There wouldn't be anyone to find you if you got lost in this meadow you call a backyard. You should carry rescue flares when you walk around out here," she told him. "You could disappear and never be heard from again."

"I'm counting on you to rescue me."

"You want me to jog up with a barrel of brandy around my neck?"

"Just bring yourself." He leaned in to brush a quick kiss over her lips. "That's all I need to revive me."

She wondered if she would ever be able to get near him without that rush in her veins. Reluctantly, she pulled away. "None of that," she said. "If you want to get this garden in today, we need to get going. It'll take a good hour or two just to clear space for the beds."

In reality, it took closer to three, between weed whacking and mowing the meadow grass and using the Rototiller to dig down to the soil. And then there was the process of getting the compost into the ground.

"How many more of these are we going to need?" Damon steered the dozenth wheelbarrow of compost to a stop by one of the vegetable beds and dumped it out.

"One more and I think that's it," Cady told him, digging it in, then raking it smooth. The ground had gone from pale and dry to rich and dark. Now, it looked like soil where seeds could grow. Of course, having Damon run a few more loads of compost over wouldn't be an entirely bad thing, she thought, watching his muscles flex under his T-shirt as he tipped the barrow up again.

There was something about a man in jeans and work boots, especially if those jeans hung just above his hips and showed off a truly excellent ass that was normally hidden by his apron and checks. And then there were those arms and shoulders. They never showed those on TV, she thought dreamily as he grabbed a shovel. Yep, add a scruffy stubble and a little bit of sweat and she was a happy girl.

Damon glanced up at her, then at the rake she leaned on. "You planning on using that anytime soon?"

"I'm busy supervising," she told him blandly.

He straightened slowly. "Supervising, huh?" He spiked his shovel into the ground.

"Sure. You don't want to make any mistakes, do you?" She watched as he walked toward her, feeling the familiar skip in her heartbeat.

"I don't know, sometimes mistakes can be interesting." He slipped his arms around her waist.

"You're distracting me from my work."

"I'm just letting you supervise from up close," he countered, locking his mouth over hers and sliding his hands down over her derriere.

How was it that he could so effortlessly heat her blood? All it took was a word, a touch, and pleasure became fierce need. All it took was a taste of him, and she found herself consumed by the demand for more.

"No." Cady forced herself to break the kiss before her will dissolved entirely. "It's already noon. If we don't keep going, we'll never get finished."

"It's going to take all afternoon?" He nibbled on her ear. "We won't have any time at all to play?"

"You were the guy who went nuts with the seeds and the pony packs. We should get to it, make sure we have time to get it all done."

"I suppose I can wait—for now."

Now it was her turn to lean in with a kiss. "You're so deprived. It'll only take a few hours."

He sighed. "Tell me what to do."

"We've probably put in enough compost for now," she allowed.

"Good news."

"For you, maybe." She picked up her rake and began smoothing the area where he'd been turning over the soil. "I kind of liked watching."

"I noticed. What?" he asked when she turned to see him standing by his shovel.

"Now who's slacking off?" And staring at her neckline in a way that made her skin heat.

"Supervising," he told her blandly.

She couldn't keep feeling this giddy bliss, Cady thought, stepping in to give him a long, lingering kiss. Like the anemic soil they'd just transformed, the part of her life that had been incomplete had somehow turned rich with affection and laughter, saturated with joy. It was just temporary, she reminded herself. She couldn't get used to it, but it was hard to remember when she felt like this. She moved away.

Damon stared. "What was that for?"

"Just checking to be sure your lips were in working order," she replied with a straight face. "All right. Grab the seeds and let's get planting."

It was one of her favorite tasks, being wrist deep in rich, dark soil. There was, in planting a garden, an optimism, a trust in the future. It was the same feeling she had seeing wrapped packages under the Christmas tree, knowing that the bare earth held the surprise of germinating seeds that would transform everything.

Damon knelt beside her. "What do we do?"

She ripped open a packet of corn seeds. "This is the easy part. Use your finger to make a little trench." She demonstrated, drawing her forefinger along the soil. "Now drop the kernels in, an inch or so apart. Push the dirt over the top and pat it down. Lightly." She caught his hand and demonstrated. When he resumed, she nodded. "You've got it," she said and moved to plant celeriac.

"So why did you get into landscaping?" Damon asked, finishing with the corn and picking up a packet of rosemary.

Cady sat back on her heels and swiped a strand of hair back with her arm. "Plants are easy. They don't pitch fits on you, they don't need to be catered to."

"Aren't you supposed to talk to them?"

"Yeah, but they don't go on and on and expect you to be interested. And they don't tend to show up four hours early for check-in." She watched him sprinkle the seeds into the earthen groove and reached over to help cover them. "Anyway, I always liked being outdoors. It used to drive me crazy, being stuck inside in summer, cleaning rooms or making breakfast or being nice to guests."

"Yeah, that being nice part, I just hate that."

She shot him a look. "Do you want to hear or do you just want to mock me?"

"I want to hear, although mocking you does have its charms."

She swatted him. "Anyway, the only break was helping my dad outside when he did handyman stuff around the place or worked on the grounds. So I started volunteering. The better I got at it, the more I got to do. At some point, I realized I had kind of a knack for it—and my parents realized it was a good way to keep guests from demanding their money back."

"Convenient," he observed.

"Very," she agreed, adding a row of cilantro.

"Did you go to a vo-tech or something to learn how it all worked?"

"No, I was more like you." She smoothed the soil. "I found somebody who was really good at it and got him to take me on. I worked for him until I figured I'd learned what I needed to know. And then I went solo a couple of years back. You're getting me at a bargain today, I hope you know."

"And I'm forever grateful for it," he said. "How's it going?"

She raised her shoulders and let them drop. "I'm paying the bills." She rose to go get the pony packs of tomato seedlings. "It would be easier if my danged boss would ever give me a raise."

"Doncha hate that?"

"She's the worst. A slave driver. All work, no fun."

"Oh, I wouldn't say that." He rose to follow her. "I wouldn't say that at all."

Cady recognized the glint in his eye. She felt the shiver down deep. "We've got tomatoes to plant," she reminded him.

"I'd hate to leave you brooding over your boss." He skimmed his hands up her sides.

"And zucchini," she added.

"In fact, I kind of like your boss," he said, nuzzling her neck.

"And thyme," she managed.

"Oh, we've got lots of time," he murmured, and drew her down to the ground.

The flattened meadow grass was soft beneath them. The sun was warm on her skin. And Damon's mouth was soft, so soft on hers.

"We shouldn't be doing this," she managed, but her fingers wound through his hair.

He teased the hem of her T-shirt from her jeans. "It's an ancient Indian fertility rite, guarantees a good harvest."

"We can't—" She groaned at the feel of his mouth on her bare nipple. "We can't make love out here. Someone could see."

"Then the neighbors will learn something," he said against her breasts.

"You don't have any neighbors," she panted as she slid her hands down into his jeans.

"Exactly," he said.

Chapter Thirteen

Damon scowled at his computer screen. Of all the many tasks his job entailed, pricing entrées had to be his least favorite. Second-least, he corrected himself. Getting harassed by Ron, the Sextant's manager, for not turning in his menu data headed the list.

When the phone rang, he reached for it impatiently. "I know. You'll have the pricing in your in-box as soon as I get it done."

There was a short silence. "Is that any way to talk to an old friend?" purred a husky voice.

Damon let out a long, slow breath. "Francesca. What a surprise to hear from you."

Francesca Cornwell, dedicated gourmet, *Chef's Challenge* judge and the fiercely ambitious editor of *Dining Well* magazine.

And, one wine-sodden night, his lover.

She was in her early forties but looked a decade younger

at first glance. She reveled in her position as an industry insider only slightly less than her ability to influence careers—for better or for worse.

"So I hear you're living up in the wilds," she said in her cut-crystal British accent.

"I'm living in Maine, yeah. And you're still in Manhattan terrorizing your staff, I assume."

"Of course. Most especially for not finding out that you were leaving. Why was I the last to hear? The least you could have done is given me a scoop."

"Why would I do that?"

"It might have made me think kindly of you. In which case I might have been calling to give you the cover of our Hot Chefs issue," she added in a tone that invited him to grovel.

Not going to happen. "My mistake," he said, instead.

"A serious one."

He heard the beep of call-waiting in his ear. Ron, he thought. "So why are you calling?"

"To tell you we've decided to put you on the cover of our Hot Chefs issue. And before you start congratulating yourself, it's not because of any of this revolutionary New England cuisine hogwash I've been hearing. The publisher's convinced that mad mug of yours sells magazines."

"You always were good for the ego, Francesca," Damon said.

"It serves you right for not telling me what you were up to." She sulked.

There was no point in observing out loud that he hadn't seen her in nearly a year. Or that he wouldn't have told her if he had.

"Just so you won't make that mistake again, I'll be up week after next to interview you. You can tell me what you're planning next."

"Maybe this is it."

She just snorted. "You have a choice of Tuesday or Wednesday."

"Either works. Tuesday's better," he said. "After lunch service."

"Then we'll be there Wednesday at 8:00 a.m."

"Sure. Come to the front desk of the inn when you get here. They'll hunt me down. You know how to find the place, right?"

"Of course. We'll see you then."

He'd had a few calls, a couple of interviews since the *Globe* review had appeared. A cover story in *Dining Well*, though, that would put him back on top. After that, it was just a matter of time before the next big offer.

Somehow, the thought didn't please him the way it had a month before.

"Hey, Chef, can I talk to you for a minute?"

It was Roman, standing outside his little office cubbyhole.

"Sure." Damon finished his e-mail to Ron and hit Send. He glanced over at the young sous chef. "What's on your mind?"

"You said you were interested in hearing ideas about new dishes."

"Yeah, sure."

"Well, I came up with one. It's a lobster clambake on a plate." Interesting. "Keep going," Damon said.

"Lobster in puff pastry, with a couple of steamers, a corn cake and a corn sauce. You juice the corn, cook it up with a little butter and lemon juice to wake it up. I figured it fit with the reworked New England thing."

"You might be onto something. How are you thinking of plating it?"

"Like that." Roman stepped aside and pointed to the counter behind him.

Damon rose and walked over. "Planning ahead, huh?"

"I figured it was easier to show you than to tell you. The lobster's from home." He handed Damon a fork. "What do you think?"

The plating worked, Damon thought, the dashes of color, the use of shapes. Then he took a bite and chewed thoughtfully, letting the flavors come together in his mouth.

Roman shifted uneasily, watching. "Okay, well, I'll leave it with you. I've got to get back to prep."

"Hang on a second." The kid was nervous, Damon realized. He'd put himself out there, taken a risk and now he was worried about the result. "So you came up with this yourself, out of the blue?"

"Yeah. Malika and I were at a clambake this weekend. I started thinking about how I could pull together all those flavors in one plate. It's just a first try," he added anxiously, though Damon was willing to bet there'd been more than a few lobsters sacrificed in Roman's kitchen already.

"It's a good first try," Damon said, reaching for another bite. "In fact, better than good. This is dynamic."

"Really? You like it?"

"Hell, yeah, I like it. Flavor profile, composition, it hits on all levels. And you can't go wrong with lobster."

"I was thinking of serving it as one of the dishes at the boss's birthday party next weekend," Roman said.

"Good idea. Work up an order list for it. We'll add it to the menu after the party, for the rest of the summer."

"You mean it?"

"Absolutely. Oh, and, Roman," he added as the sous chef started to turn away, "keep thinking. I want another special from you for next month. Now get back to prep," he growled.

He turned back to his office as Roman headed back to the line. A few minutes later, Damon heard the back door swing open and slam, and then very faintly, a whoop of triumph.

And he grinned to himself. This was what it was about, he thought. Not Francesca and her games but a clambake on a plate and a kid who was just learning to trust his talent.

* * *

Cady stood at her workbench in the greenhouse. Midday sun streamed in through the roof. She sang along with the Dixie Chicks on her music player while she finished seeding the trays of microgreens before her.

A sound at the door had her stomach fluttering. It was midafternoon, far enough after lunch service to be the right time. Damon had taken to stopping in to see her afternoons on the days she worked the grounds, and she'd taken to being there. She turned, expecting him.

Instead, she saw her mother.

"Oh, Mom. Hi."

"Hi." Amanda stepped inside.

A party update, Cady figured. "So, I think Max and I have everything all set for next weekend," she said. "Roman's got the menu finalized, Damon signed off on it."

"Good. Your aunt Barbara and uncle Michael are coming up next Friday. I've put them at the inn out on the highway. Everyone else is close enough to drive in for the party, except Walker and his wife."

"Dad already knows Max and Walker are coming for the weekend, so we're cool there."

Amanda waved a hand. "I don't think he's been paying close enough attention to notice anything anyway, as busy as he's been with all this traffic at the inn."

"All we've got to do is keep the secret this weekend and next week."

"I'll be glad when it's over. Keeping secrets is exhausting. Isn't it?" She looked at Cady deliberately.

Cady frowned. "What are you talking about?"

Amanda hesitated. "Are you having an affair with Damon Hurst?"

The answer, she was sure, was all over her face, but she nodded. "Yes."

"This whole time?"

"No. It's pretty recent. Sudden. I wasn't expecting it but we…" She took a breath. "This is kind of a strange conversation to have with your mother."

"It's kind of a strange conversation to be having with your daughter," Amanda returned.

"Then why are we having it?"

Amanda closed her eyes and shook her head. "Do you remember a month ago, we were standing in our kitchen and you were telling your father and I what a mess Damon Hurst made of his personal life?"

"And I remember you telling me he'd changed."

"Enough to run our restaurant. Not enough that I want my daughter sleeping with him."

"Mom." Cady met her eyes steadily. "I know I said those things and I believed them at the time. I don't anymore. He's been here, what, six weeks now? I've watched him, I've spent time with him. He's not the person they talk about."

"They can't all be stories."

"No, they can't. But didn't you tell me once that people grow up? I believe he has." She paused. "I believe in him."

Amanda let out a long breath. "I'm sorry. I know you're an adult, and I know it's not my business. But I seem to remember you telling me that you couldn't help worrying about your father and me." Her eyes softened. "I can't help worrying about you. You're my daughter and I want you to be happy. I just don't know that he's the person who can make you that way."

"Didn't you used to tell me I was the only one who could make myself happy?"

"And are you?"

Cady looked at her mother. "I think I might be."

"You've always kept yourself closed off from almost every-

body." Amanda blinked a few times. "It's not good for you.
You need someone to bring you out of yourself. I don't know,
maybe Damon can do that. You've been different the last
couple of weeks. I noticed it, I just didn't think to wonder why.
Maybe I should have asked."

"We would just have had this conversation earlier."

"What an usually diplomatic way for you to tell me it's
none of my business," Amanda said with a watery laugh.
"Maybe he's a good influence on you after all."

"We'll find out," Cady said, hugging her. "We'll find out."

The morning was cool, dew still on the leaves as Damon
stood in his backyard, spraying the vegetable beds. Or what
Cady assured him were vegetable beds. You couldn't prove it
by him. The tomatoes and peppers they'd planted as seedlings
still sat inside their hot caps, looking as if a row of scarecrows
had been buried so that only the tops of their hats showed. Otherwise, just like every morning in the week since they'd planted
the garden, he was just watering dirt as far as he could tell.

Still, the air was sweet and the water coming out of the
sprayer looked like a shower of golden needles in the morning
light. Patience, he reminded himself. It had taken weeks for
the restaurant review, too. Just as it would take weeks more
for the seeds of the *Globe* story to bear fruit. Sure, business
at the restaurant had picked up almost instantly, but for him
personally, nothing had changed except the call from Francesca for *Dining Well*, and that interview wouldn't see the
light of day for a month or more. Things took time.

And things took time with Cady. A week had passed since
they'd first slept together. Or had sex, he corrected himself.
They hadn't ever actually slept the night through. On the
couple of nights they'd managed to get together, she'd always
insisted on going home or sending him back to his place.
There were the excuses—they had to get up early, she didn't

want to be carting a bag of clothes around, but he knew that wasn't the reason.

She was holding back.

It was early, he told himself. There was no logical reason he should press. He'd always been the king of the speed affair and alarmed by women who wanted to glom on to him. He should have been relieved she wanted to play it casual.

Why, then, did it frustrate him?

"Well, if it isn't the gentleman gardener."

He glanced over to see Cady coming to him across the lawn and felt the glad rush, the rightness at having her there. Whether she'd stayed over or just driven there, she was with him now. Sure, it was only a Sunday stolen away for the two of them but it was time and it was theirs.

"Nice to see you're being diligent." She stopped next to him.

"Twice a day, every day, even if I do have to drag my sorry ass out here at night after I get home from the restaurant." He curved one arm around her waist to pull her in for a kiss.

"You wanted the garden, you got the garden," she told him. "Anyway, once they get established, you can scale it back to every couple of days."

"Assuming they ever sprout. How do I know the seeds were any good?"

"I wouldn't have picked you for a pessimist, Hurst. You should have more faith."

He leaned in to nuzzle her neck. "Did you bring clothes so you could stay?"

"Tomorrow's Monday, remember? It might be your Sunday, but for the rest of us poor schleps, Monday's the start of the workweek."

A logical enough explanation, still… "It would be nice to have you here in the morning, one of these times."

"Then we'll have to work on that," she said, kissing him.

It wasn't an empty promise, Cady told herself. She just had

to get to the point she could. What was between them was nothing she'd expected, nothing she'd gone looking for. A month before, Damon Hurst had only existed as a distant and improbable presence on television. She'd never in a million years expected to ever see him, let alone be spending time in his bed—or any man's bed, for that matter.

And that was the problem. She needed to catch up. It was extraordinary to believe that this was her life. When he slipped his arms around her and pressed his mouth to hers, it felt like the most natural thing on earth. The rest of the time, it simply seemed impossible.

In a way, she felt as though she was living a double life. There were the hours she spent at the Compass Rose, and with her family, and then there were the precious hours when it was only Damon and her and she felt herself turn liquid in his arms. In some ways, it was the easiest thing she'd ever done. In some ways, it was the hardest.

The rave reviews continued to come in. The Sextant was suddenly a destination for foodies—and for food groupies who were there purely for Damon. The glamorous, beautiful groupies who ordered the chef's tasting so that they could meet and flirt with him.

It was hard for Cady to put it out of her mind. The two of them had gotten involved when he had been flying under the radar, when his focus had been on the Compass Rose and the Sextant. And her. Now, he was being pulled in a dozen different directions at once. Now, everybody seemed to want a piece of him. And although it didn't seem to bother him, it just made Cady uneasy.

She couldn't compete with the groupies. She couldn't compete with the women from his past—and she didn't want to. Sure, she loved the meals he cooked for her but she was equally happy with pizza and beer. She wasn't part of the high-powered world he was used to. He seemed to have changed, but what if the real Damon came out now that the cult of personality had reformed? What if the man she'd known for the previous month was just Damon on downtime and the things he seemed to want—Grace Harbor, the Sextant, her—were forgotten? He would go on and be fine, but if she gave him everything, she wasn't at all sure how she'd survive.

And so she tried to keep a small bit of distance between them. She tried to remind herself that it wouldn't last. It was only a matter of time, and if she were smart, she'd enjoy it while she could.

This was the man who hadn't spoken to his father in almost a decade. This was a man who could leave the past behind without missing a beat. If she were smart, she'd run as far and as fast and as hard from him as she could. But standing like this, with her arms around him and her head on his shoulder, it all felt right. And she was powerless to do anything but stay.

"Cady."

She raised her head. There was a note in Damon's voice, an intensity, a barely suppressed excitement. When she turned and looked to where he was pointing, she understood why. She saw what she would swear hadn't been there just a moment before. Saw, perhaps, the answer to her questions. Coming out of the ground in barely visible filaments were the green shoots of dill and cilantro, celery and corn. And thyme.

And thyme.

The seeds they had planted together were sprouting.

Chapter Fourteen

Keeping the grounds of the Compass Rose perfect was Cady's job. Knowing that family and friends were coming to visit was a whole different thing from anonymous guests, though. She'd spent the better part of the week manicuring the property, making sure everything was immaculate.

And now, at midday on Friday, she needed more time.

She crossed the back lawn of the inn to drop a rake in the toolshed, automatically waving to her father, out on the lawn. Then her footsteps slowed as she took a closer look. He wasn't talking to a guest as she'd so often seen him doing. He wasn't repairing a railing or walkway. He was just sitting in one of the Adirondack chairs on the grass, looking out at the water.

"What are you doing here, you slacker?" She walked behind him to rub his shoulders. "People see you sitting around too much, they're going to start talking."

"I'm trying to decide whether I like the harbor better in the morning or the afternoon."

"You have to pick one or the other?"

"It seems like the kind of thing I should know. I've been here long enough."

There was a strange note in his voice that had her looking at him more carefully. "This wouldn't have anything to do with your birthday, would it?"

He put a hand over hers. "That obvious, is it?"

"Lucky guess." She sat down next to him.

"It's always the birthdays with the zeros in them that make you take stock," he said.

"I'd say you'd have to come out pretty well in any stock-taking," she said. "Beautiful wife, three good kids, if you ignore that incident with the lobster pots and the outboard— I mean, how was I supposed to know that Tucker had tuned the throttle? Anyway, look around," she said, emboldened by his faint smile. "You've got this beautiful inn that's a national historic landmark, you live on the water, everybody in town knows your name and respects you.

"And speaking of the inn," she continued, "you also have a good head for business. Your gamble with Damon Hurst paid off. Mom says reservations have been going through the roof. Your chef's going to be the cover story of some high-powered food magazine. It's all coming together."

"So what?"

"So what?"

"What does it matter? So we make it a success. Then what do we do, turn around and sell it off to the highest bidder to do whatever they want with it?" There was something almost angry in his voice.

Cady blinked. "Well, no."

"We can't work it the rest of our lives. Who's going to take it over? You?"

"I'm not—"

"Exactly. And the other two don't even live around here."

"Maybe Tucker wants it."

"Tucker's already got two businesses. You know what it's like here, you know it's a full-time job." He stopped and gave a dispirited sigh. "Ah, don't listen to me, I'm just running off at the mouth. It's just that some days I get up and wish I could just relax with a cup of coffee."

She put a hand on his leg. "You know, you could hire a manager."

"The Compass Rose has always been a family business. That's part of what makes it different."

"I'm not saying you change that. I'm just saying bring in a person who can take some of the load so that you can afford to take a vacation, have the weekends off, God forbid. You can still be around and do what you've always done. Just less of it, that's all," she finished.

"I don't know," he said doubtfully.

"It can't hurt to check into it, can it?"

He considered. "Maybe once we get our finances back into shape, I'll look around."

But the inn, she knew, was just a part of what was bothering him. "Dad, I know having a birthday with a round number is a wake-up call, but…it's just a number. It's not you."

"Oh, trust me, sweetheart—" he shook his head in amusement "—it's not just a number. My back and my hands remind me of that all the time."

"Sure, but you know what? When you're seventy, you're going to look back on today and say, 'Man, sixty was great. I wish I were sixty again.' And at eighty, you're going to look back at seventy. It's always going to be that way," she said, warming to her subject. "The thing to do is enjoy where you're at when you're there. And know that there are a hell of a lot of people out there who love you." She leaned over to kiss his cheek. "Including me."

"And me right back at you." He stroked her hair for a moment, then slapped his thighs and stood up. "You know what? You're right. I guess that means I'd better get making the most of fifty-nine while I've still got it."

Cady grinned. "Go, Daddy, go."

"Nice job with the lobster trio."

Damon looked up from scrubbing the counter to see a tall, sinewy man leaning against the doorway, surveying the kitchen. His cropped hair was dirty blond, his face weathered. His gaze wasn't cynical, exactly, so much as calculating and unflinching. He scanned everything, missed little.

He never had.

"Hello, Jack," Damon said to his onetime partner. "Looking to open up an outpost in Maine?"

Jack Worth grinned and calculation became affability. "I wanted to come see the superstar at work."

Damon's gaze was steady. "Time was you didn't have to come to Maine for that." Time was, they'd worked side by side, night after night, building an empire. Damon had been the food and the face of Pommes de Terre; Jack had been the moneyman, the guy behind the scenes. They'd hatched big plans over cognac at the bar of the closed restaurant: a bigger location when the lease was up at the end of the year, a second restaurant in the Meatpacking District.

But then had come the television success and with it, the fizzy bubbles of fame that had floated Damon's feet off the ground. There weren't enough hours in the day for the things he needed to do, let alone wanted. Days in the studio and late nights in the kitchen had bled into early mornings in the clubs. And it became harder and harder to remember what really mattered.

When the Cooking Channel had canceled his show, it had

almost been a relief. He could focus again, could go back to what really mattered, which was the food. Instead, Jack had called him into his office and broken the news: he wasn't renewing the lease. They weren't moving, they weren't opening up a second location. He was closing the restaurant and ending their partnership.

Free fall had begun.

Damon looked now into those gray eyes. Jack had succeeded in the restaurant business for almost twenty years because he was willing to do what was necessary. His had been the final rejection, the final betrayal. And yet it had also been the start of the way back.

Standing before him now, Damon wasn't sure what to feel. "Manhattan to Maine. It's a long way to come for lunch."

"It was worth it, though. You haven't lost your touch."

Damon tossed the sponge back in the bucket. "That's a relief."

"People are talking, you know."

"About me?"

"Who else? You always were one for reinventing yourself, but this is a strange choice, even for you."

There were eyes on him, Damon reminded himself, and a dozen pairs of ears pricked up to hear what came next. "I need a break," he said. "Let's go take a walk."

It was one of those near-perfect days, warm without being hot, the air off the ocean soft and sweet. They walked to the edge of the property, looking down to where the calm waters of the harbor lapped against the stone breakwater. "God's country, up here," Jack observed.

"This, coming from the man who swore Manhattan was the center of the universe?"

"Manhattan *is* the center of the universe," Jack replied. "That doesn't mean I can't appreciate a place like this. After all, you can."

"Thanks for the compliment."

"You're out in the sticks, no doubt about it. You've got a decent kitchen and a staff that appears to know what it's doing. But it's strictly small-time."

"What about you? You're out of the business."

Jack snorted. "I'll never be out of the business. I have other restaurants. I just shut down Pommes de Terre because you were beginning to be too much of a pain in the ass. There's no one as talented as you in the kitchen, you know that, but talent isn't always enough."

"Did you come up here to lecture me?" Damon asked with a little edge in his voice.

"No. I admit, I'm curious to know just how long you plan to continue this little…exercise. Or have you lost your nerve and decided to make it long-term?"

"Lost my nerve?"

"You could have found a job in Manhattan if you'd wanted one. More eyes on you there, though. Your missteps would be more public. So you come up here to do your finger exercises, figure out if you've still got what it takes."

"Is that what I'm doing?" Damon said drily. "Thanks for clarifying that."

"Anytime. And it looks like a tight operation. After the meal I had, I'm sure you'll get the reviews in *New York* magazine and the *Times*."

"And *Dining Well*. Francesca called me a couple of days ago about doing an interview."

"Ah, the black widow spider," Jack said. "Watch out for that one or you're likely to find out she's dining well on you."

"She says she's giving me the cover on her Hot Chefs issue."

"Congratulations. But the place still isn't enough. What can you do, a hundred, hundred and fifty covers a night if you're lucky? It's small-time. And if you stick here, you're going to be small-time, too."

Damon frowned. "Whoa, Trigger. Slow down. You're

getting way ahead of things. I'm here and I'm cooking, that's it."

"A Michelin-starred chef working at a country inn?"

"For the time being. It's letting me concentrate on what I want. The day it stops seeming like the best thing to do, I move on."

"So it's just a stopover?"

"Call it what you want. I figure I'll work here for a year or two, get my chops back, and when I find the right opportunity, I'll move on." It was the plan, as it had been from the beginning.

So why did he suddenly feel guilty saying it?

Across the lawn, he saw Cady coming toward him over the grass, carrying her cell phone. She wore shorts that showed off those gorgeous legs and a T-shirt the color of olives that brought out the green in her eyes.

"I'm sorry to interrupt," she began.

"Not a problem," Damon said easily. "This is an old friend. Cady, meet Jack Worth. Jack's up from Manhattan. He and I were partners in the restaurant business back in the day. Jack, this is Cady McBain. Her parents own the Compass Rose."

Jack was already reaching for her hand. "Pleased to meet you."

She looked at him just a fraction of a second too long before shaking. "Nice to meet you, too."

"Your parents have a beautiful place here. I see you can take credit for some of that." He nodded at the gardening gloves in her pocket.

"I just work here. The rest of it is all them." She smiled faintly. "And our rock star chef."

Jack glanced over at Damon. "Sounds like she's got your number, bud."

"Listen, I won't keep you. Damon, Max is on the phone asking if we need anything from Portland before she heads out of town."

"Nothing I can think of," he said.

Cady nodded. "All right, I'll let you guys get back to it. Jack, it was nice to meet you. Have a safe trip back home."

She walked away, cell phone back to her ear. And Damon watched her the whole time.

"Not your usual type," Jack observed.

Damon turned to him. "What's that supposed to mean?"

"Is this part of the new you, the wholesome small-town girl thing? I got to say, like her a lot better than some of the fashion victims you used to run around with."

"Why are you here, Jack?" Even he could hear the sharpness in his voice. "It's a long way to come just for lunch, and it isn't just a friendly visit to see how I'm doing."

"Maybe it is."

"Someone once told me there are no friends in this business, only people you do business with. I believe that was you, Jack."

"You believe wrong," Jack shot back at him. "We were friends, until you went spinning off the edge."

"And you were happy enough to give me a push."

"Do you really think I wanted to do that?" The gray eyes iced over to pewter. "I walked away from a hell of a lot of money closing Pommes de Terre. If it had been just business, I would have kept raking in the dough and let you keep throwing your life down the toilet, and when you finally crashed and burned, brought in a sous chef to do the work for you. I closed the restaurant because it was the only thing I could think of that might wake you up. Talking sure as hell hadn't. At that point you didn't know who your friends were. It looks like maybe you still don't."

He stalked away.

"Jack, wait."

"What?" He stopped and turned to face Damon again, his expression closed. "Make it quick. I've got a long drive."

"Look." Damon put his hands on his hips and looked down,

then raised his head to meet Jack's gaze. "A lot's gone on in the past two years. I know I screwed up toward the end of our partnership and I'm sorry. We made a good team."

"We did."

"Maybe we could again, sometime."

"Maybe sooner than later." It was Jack's turn to pause. "That's part of why I came up here, to talk to you, but now I'm wondering if I should bother."

"What do you mean?" Damon asked.

"It depends."

"Depends on what?"

"On whether I can depend on you." Those gray eyes assessed him. "Can I do that?"

And Damon had a sense of his future hanging in the air before him. Did he reach out for it or not? Slowly, he nodded. "Yeah. Yeah, you can. What's on your mind?"

"I've been in some negotiations with Dimitri Stephanopolous."

Damon stared. "Dimitri Stephanopolous?"

"You've heard of him?"

"Who hasn't?" The single biggest developer on the globe, with properties on every continent. Currently building the world's biggest resort in Dubai, Damon recalled reading. "What are you doing with him?"

"He opened a new casino in Vegas last summer. Fifty stories, twenty-eight hundred rooms." Jack turned to watch Cady water the flower baskets hanging from the edge of the porch. "It's got four upscale restaurants and every one of them is hemorrhaging money. He's brought me on board to turn that around."

The hair on the back of Damon's neck prickled. "And?"

Jack's eyes cut back to him. "I want you to be my executive chef. This is the big one, Damon. If we get a foothold in the Stephanopolous empire, we grow as it grows. We turn

Pommes de Terres into an international brand. You could be the next Todd English or Wolfgang Puck, if you keep your head on straight. Are you interested?"

It was what he'd been waiting for. It was bigger than he'd ever imagined. "It depends. I want to know more about it. I also want to know more about this Stephanopolous character, assuming he's the one I'd be dealing with."

"You'd be dealing with me. They've given me full authority over the restaurants—in writing, I might add."

Damon smiled faintly. "I would have expected nothing less." Jack Worth was the one restaurateur in Manhattan nobody ever tried to cheat, and for good reason. "What are you going to do about all those restaurants you're talking about in New York?"

Jack shrugged. "Keep making money off of them. I figure with the right executive chef out in Vegas, I only need to be out there half-time. The right executive chef," he repeated. "Of course, that executive chef would have to live there. I'd figured you'd be a natural for it." He glanced over at Cady again. "That was before I realized you might be settling down."

Damon's gaze followed Jack's. Cady reached up to water another basket, her hair glinting red in the sunlight, her body lithe and strong. He remembered what it was like to hold her in the moonlight. He wondered what it would be like to wake with her in his arms.

"I never really thought it would happen with you," Jack said.

"Huh?" Damon turned to him.

"She's got you, doesn't she?"

Damon's eyes narrowed. "Did you come here to offer me a job or talk about my personal life?"

"Maybe a little of both."

"Stick to Vegas," Damon advised. "My personal life is under control."

"Whatever you say. Think it over this weekend," Jack said. "I'll give you a call next week." He gave Cady another glance. "Just a stopover," he repeated. "Remember that."

"Thanks for letting me stay with you," Max told Cady as she set down her garment bag. "Although maybe thanks is overstating the case." Putting her hands on her hips, she surveyed the controlled chaos of the living room.

"Hey, I put fresh sheets on the hide-a-bed and I cleaned the bathroom," Cady said. "And I'm saving you from spending two days in the same house as Walker's wife."

"Leaving Mom and Dad to deal with her."

"Elise isn't so bad with them. You're the one who seems to bring out her claws."

"That's because she knows I see through her."

"I think she's jealous," Cady countered. "Or intimidated. She can spend money all day—"

"And does," Max put in.

"—on clothes and makeup," Cady continued with a grin, "and never come close to looking as good as you do."

"And there are plenty of people out there that put me in the same spot," Max said. "I don't know why she's so hung up on it. We don't even live in the same city for God's sakes."

Cady shrugged. She'd long ago solved the issue of how to compete with Max by choosing not to. Being herself, for better or worse, was far easier.

"Anyway," Max continued, "how I look or how Elise looks isn't important—"

"Tell that to her."

"I just don't like the way she treats Walker."

"That makes two of us. You want something to drink, by the way? Coke? Snapple?"

"Zinfandel? Cabernet?" Max slipped her shoes off and stretched luxuriously. "Getting out of Portland on a Friday is bad enough, but then there's all the weekender traffic to fight getting here. It took me almost two hours."

"Just wait until July," Cady said.

"Oh, great, something to look forward to."

"Hey, you're here. Kick back and relax. We don't have anything to do until tomorrow." Cady walked into the kitchen, then popped her head back out. "I forgot, I actually do have some wine. Damon left a bottle last time he was here."

"'The last time he was here'? Your saucepan jockey has seen this place?"

Cady stuck her head out of the kitchen and grinned. "Twice. He even made dinner last time, which is why the wine."

"Now that's love."

"Oh, well, I don't know about that," she said uncomfortably.

"Relax." Max leaned against the wall at the entry to the kitchen. "I was just joking. Do Mom and Dad know?"

"Mom's figured it out," Cady said, pouring the wine into juice glasses.

"It's pretty hard to get anything past her. I never managed it in high school, anyway." Max eyed her glass. "You know, you can buy actual wine goblets at a discount store for a few dollars."

"Yeah, but these have character." Cady walked past her into the living room.

"Is that what that's called?" Max followed her. "So Mom figured it out?"

"She saw him coming out of the greenhouse after we'd been fooling around."

Max raised a brow as she dropped to the couch next to Cady. "Fooling around with a little *f* or a big *f*?"

"Little *f*," Cady retorted. "Jeez, give me a little bit of credit for having a brain."

"Just asking," Max said. "It was still kind of taking a chance if you were trying to keep things quiet."

"I know." Cady's gaze flicked up to the ceiling. "He'd just come by to say hi and we got a little carried away."

"Ah, young love." Max clacked her glass against Cady's. "Here's to fooling around. So how is it going?"

"I don't know. Okay, I guess."

"You guess?"

"Well, it's hardly gotten started."

"Are you kidding? You guys just got involved. The time's like dog years. It's been, what, three weeks? That's like the equivalent of a decade or two."

"Well, yeah, but considering the hours we both work, it doesn't translate into a whole lot of time together. I have Saturdays off, he doesn't. He has Mondays off, I work. We both get Sundays off but that's about it. And he's at the restaurant every night besides that until eleven or twelve."

"Which shouldn't stop a pair of determined love bunnies," Max pointed out.

Cady rolled her eyes. "It's not just about the sex part, you know. I mean, the sex part's good—"

"Good?" Max raised a brow.

"Well, phenomenal." Enough to give her a little buzz just at the thought. "I mean, yeah, it amazes me every time. It seems like the most incredible thing in the world that we get to keep doing it again and again. But I just…"

"Just what?"

"I just wish we had more time to be together. We have to be careful around the inn, and after Mom saw us in the green house, I feel like we can't be alone there, either." She shook her head. "Then again, it's a hell of a lot more than I've ever had with any other guy, ever. The way he makes me feel… Sometimes I look in the mirror and I can't stop smiling because I just can't believe it's actually happening to me."

"You ask me," Max said, "it's long past time that the male population figured out what a hot number you are."

"I don't need the whole population." Cady sighed. "I just need one." The right one.

"I'll see what I can do about that." Max looked at her assessingly. "What are you planning to wear to the party?"

"Oh, I don't know. My black jacket and pants, probably."

"To your father's sixtieth birthday party?"

"It's all I have," Cady defended. "And I don't have the kind of money to blow on something dressy to wear once."

"If you bought the right thing, you'd wear it more than once."

"Max, I am not going shopping."

"Ah, now we get down to the real reason." Max rose and went to rummage around in her garment bag. "You're lucky you have a big sister who loves you. Aha!" She pulled out a swatch of brilliantly colored fabric swathed in plastic. "Here we go."

Cady's policy was generally to be suspicious of any clothing that came in dry-cleaning bags. "What's that, a dress?"

"You did wear them, last time I checked."

"Sometimes." Mostly when forced. "It's not one of those tight things you always wear, right? And no heels?" It wasn't dressing up she objected to, per se, it was the time it took to do it and then being uncomfortable in clothing she couldn't move in.

Max glanced at her, amused. "Don't worry. It's not too tight and not too short. And no heels because mine wouldn't fit you. Sandals will do, if you have them." She held the dress up against Cady. "Yep, perfect with your eyes. We'll just take care of your makeup and do your hair. Your saucepan jockey won't know what hit him."

"That's what I'm afraid of," Cady mumbled.

Chapter Fifteen

Saturday dawned brilliant and clear. By the time they got over to the Compass Rose, it was the middle of the day—as Cady had feared, there turned out to be shopping after all. They parked down by their parents' house, not wanting to take a spot in the crowded guest lot. Indeed, as they were getting out of Max's car to walk to their parents' house, a sleek, graphite-colored convertible pulled up beside them.

"Excuse me, can I leave my car here?" the dark-haired driver asked.

"Guest parking is back by the inn," Cady told him.

Ignoring her, he turned off his engine.

"Freaking guests," Cady muttered to Max. "You're going to have to move your car, sir," she said more loudly as the man got out. "This area is for family only."

He stared down at her from behind his expensive mirrored sunglasses. "How do you know I'm not?"

"Because family shows up more than once a year, Walker, you dolt," she said and launched herself at him for a hug. He might have looked like a summer person but he was, and always would be, her big brother, Grace Harbor born and bred. And for all that he was only down in Manhattan, they saw each other far too seldom. He looked thinner, she saw, and careworn in some indefinable way.

"Hey, Cades, how's tricks?" he asked, giving her a dim version of the smile that had broken girls' hearts from the time he was young.

She wondered, but decided not to ask just then. "I'm good. How about you?"

The answer to that question had once been a no-brainer. Walker had been the success story of the family, the one who'd gone to the Ivy League school, gotten the scholarships, the hot Wall Street job. Marrying into a wealthy family seemed only par for the course.

Even if his bride had been the boss's daughter.

"I'm hanging in there. Hey, Max," he said, hugging her in turn.

"Hey." She studied him. "You're looking a little rode hard and put away wet."

"Gee, you look good, too," he said wryly.

"Where's Elise?" Cady asked. "I thought she was coming, too."

"She had other things going on."

Max crossed her arms. "Other things than her father-in-law's sixtieth birthday?"

"Yeah, well, you know how it goes."

"No, but I can imagine."

"I'll tell her you sent your love," Walker said.

Max's lips twitched. "You do that."

He ran his fingers through his cropped hair and circled his shoulders.

"Long drive?" Cady asked.

"New York seems farther away from Grace Harbor than it used to."

"Continental drift," she told him.

He smiled briefly. "That must be it. So how are the rental units doing? Is Dad still in the dark about the hoedown?"

Cady glanced at the house ahead. "So far, and I don't think he's faking."

"That would be something if we could surprise him."

"I think he's been distracted. Worried about the inn and maybe a little down over turning sixty."

"Beats the alternative," Walker observed. "Is he over at the inn now?"

Cady shook her head. "Mom's got him working on the boiler in the basement. We wanted to keep him out of the way so he doesn't get it in his head to go over to the restaurant."

"What's the plan to get him there for the party?"

"I'm going to go get him right before we start and fake him out with a story about a broken pipe or something," Cady said.

"My idea," Max put in.

"I always knew you were devious." He ducked as she swatted at him. "So you walk in and everybody pops out of the woodwork and yells surprise."

"Not so loud," Cady said. "We're getting close to the house. I'll go in and get Mom and Dad." She hurried down the walk and up the steps.

Walker shook his head. "She never runs down, does she?"

"Sooner or later, we all do," Max said.

He stopped for a minute on the front walk as though wanting to put off the moment of seeing his parents.

"So what's really going on?" Max asked quietly. Only a year apart, she and Walker had been inseparable growing up, climbing trees, making forts, beaning each other with snowballs and water balloons. The frequency of snowball fights had lessened as they grew up, but the closeness had remained.

At least until Walker had married Elise Barrett.

Now, Walker jammed his hands in his pockets and stared over at the water. "Things aren't great."

"Work or home? Or both?"

"They kind of go hand in hand, don't they?"

"You tell me."

He shook his head, leaned down to pick up a rock and throw it toward the water. "You know, we always fought fair, you and I. We might have had some knock-down-drag-outs, but we never drew blood."

"Except for the time I punched you in the nose." Max studied her nails.

"You got lucky."

"Nevertheless. So what are you guys fighting about?"

"There needs to be a reason?"

It was supposed to be a joke. It wasn't supposed to sound hollow down beneath. For a moment, Walker was silent. Then he turned toward the steps. "Ah, it's no big deal. We'll work it out." He flashed a smile that didn't last long enough. "Let's forget about it all and just have a good time."

Damon strode through the kitchen like a general on inspection. "Okay, people, thirty minutes and counting. English—" he turned to the Leeds-born chef who worked the appetizer station "—where are we at on apps?"

"The crab cakes, Thai shrimp and the portabella in puff pastry are all done." English pointed to the sheet pans of hors d'oeuvres sitting on the central counter.

"The tuna crostini?"

"Just finishing the bread and they'll be ready to assemble."

It was one thing to do one hundred and fifty covers spread out over the course of a night. It was another thing entirely to serve a four-course meal to fifty-some-odd people simultaneously. And while Damon had left the planning of the party in Roman's hands, Roman hadn't worked five-hundred-plate charity benefits the way he had. When the sous chef had asked for help earlier that morning, Damon had been happy to step in.

"Okay, let's start getting the apps on serving platters for the waiters. Roman, how are we doing on the entrées?"

"The lobsters are prepped, the duck is in the *sous vide*. I'm searing off the pork now."

"Sauces all done?"

"Yes, Chef."

"Good. Rosalie, salads and soup?"

"Ready to go, Chef."

He'd had teams with better pedigrees, perhaps, but none who'd worked so hard and with so little complaint. Every one of them had shown up early that day, pleased to be helping out with Ian McBain's birthday dinner. Fondness for the man permeated the staff but it was more than that—it was a happy kitchen in general, completely lacking the flavor of ruthless ambition and backbiting Damon had encountered in other restaurants.

If he left, Damon thought, he'd miss them.

If he left.

It wasn't the time to be thinking about Jack Worth's offer, but it was hard not to. In one way, it was like being handed a gift. Sure, there'd been a time when the term "Vegas cuisine" had been a punch line but that time was long past. Casinos and restaurateurs alike had figured out that people came to the city with money to spend and that rather than blow it on roast beast and baked ziti in some buffet, many of them were happy to pay for serious food. Le Cirque, Aureole, Nobu—some of the finest restaurants in the world had opened outposts in Las Vegas. He could do worse that throw his own hand in.

But it was the greater opportunity that made his mouth go dry. A foothold in the Stephanopolous empire was very probably the biggest chance he would ever have, career wise. Restaurants around the world, international board meetings, spin-off companies…

In comparison, Grace Harbor and the world of the Compass Rose seemed very small. A Michelin-starred chef working at a country inn, Jack had said.

And yet, he'd been happy there. Day after day, for the past two months, he'd woken up smiling and eager to get started. Day after day, he'd felt a part of something very like family. Grace Harbor had brought a satisfaction to his life he hadn't realized he was missing.

And it had brought Cady.

It was right between them. He didn't understand it and it certainly wasn't anything he'd expected, but the relationship made him feel better than anything ever had. And he wasn't at all sure that he was ready to walk away from it. Or her.

Stephanopolous, the casino, the restaurants—the opportunity for money, challenge, influence. Just thinking about the possibilities made his head spin. It was a chance to do huge things, a chance to build the empire he and Jack had always talked about, a chance to live the dream.

The only problem was, he wasn't sure it was still his dream.

He shook his head. Later, he told himself. He'd figure it out later.

"Now, what happened again?" Ian asked as he followed Cady through the afternoon shadows to the restaurant.

Excitement bubbled through her, but she kept her voice modulated to concern and frustration. "The fire alarm just started going off and it won't stop. There's no smell of smoke or anything, and we've already called the fire department.

We've tried to reset it but no luck. We thought maybe you could figure it out."

"Christ on a crutch, can't I have one blessed day without something going wrong?" he demanded as they walked into the Sextant. "Your mother's trying to cook a nice dinner, all you kids are here, all dressed up. It was going to be a nice night. Just once I'd like to—"

"Surprise!"

The chorus was deafening. People were packed in the waiting area and clear back into the dining room itself.

Ian's jaw dropped. For a moment, he just stared, his expression flashing from shock to amazement to delight. "Well I'll be a sonofagun," he burst out. "What are all you people doing here?"

"Happy birthday," someone shouted.

Ian turned in a circle, grinning like a madman. "Barbara, Mike, you're supposed to be in Georgia."

"We figured we could take a break for a special occasion," his sister told him as they hugged.

He worked his way through the crowd, shaking hands and laughing before turning back to Cady and Amanda and Max. "Am I right in thinking you're the three responsible for this?"

"It was Cady's idea," Amanda said.

"We all worked on it," Cady countered.

"Thank you." Ian came over and pulled her close. "I suppose you knew all about this yesterday when I was being a sad sack," he murmured.

She gave him a smacking kiss. "I don't remember anyone being a sad sack. I just remember talking with my favorite dad."

"I'm your only dad."

"Well, how about that?"

Grinning, he hugged her again, scooping in Max and Amanda while he was at it.

"Somebody get this man a drink," Walker called and the music started up.

It was the best kind of party, one where enough of the guests knew each other to make conversation easy and enough of them didn't to keep things interesting. Jokes flew thick and fast, and if reunited friends got a little teary eyed, nobody commented. They were too busy savoring the appetizers, each more decadent than the last.

"Oh my God," Tania said, "these shrimp things are to die for."

"You said that about the crab cakes," Cady observed.

"And the crostini," Walker contributed.

"In fact, I think you've said that about every appetizer you've tasted. And you're still breathing." Cady shook her head. "How much of a miracle is that?"

"That's one word for it," Walker said, deadpan.

Tania eyed him. "I'd watch it, Walker McBain. I know where your skeletons are buried. But I'll forgive you if you bring me another martini."

Just then, there was a clinking of knives against glasses as Ian McBain got up on a chair. "Hey, everyone, can I have your attention? I'd like to make a toast," he said, straining to be heard over the hubbub.

"Pipe down!" his brother-in-law, Mike, boomed. "The man's trying to talk."

The room quieted until finally everyone was listening. Ian cleared his throat. "First, I'd like to thank everyone for coming."

"Sounds like you're trying to shoo us out before dinner," someone called out.

Ian grinned. "If you know what's good for you, you'll stay, because we've got about the best chefs in the world here. Anyway, it's not every day a man turns sixty. It's enough to make a guy think. But as a very wise person told me yesterday—" Cady saw him flick her a glance "—what matters is not the numbers, it's the good things in your life. So here's to counting my blessings—all of you here tonight, and especially my beautiful wife and my three great kids. Oh, and the staff here at Compass Rose who helped pull this off. I'm a lucky, lucky man. Here's to all of you."

He was drowned out by the chorus of cheers and the sound of dozens of glasses tapping together and the music rose.

There were moments in life, Cady thought, that were just about perfect. A bubble of pure happiness began to swell in her chest.

Tania elbowed Cady. "Speaking of things to die for, here's one coming your way."

She looked, and the bubble threatened to lift her off her feet.

After the furious intensity of the kitchen, to walk into the dining room was to relax. And to smile. On the dance floor, Ian McBain whirled his laughing wife around to "Do You Believe in Magic?" by the Lovin' Spoonful. Nearby, a pair of women, obviously longtime friends, toasted each other. In the corner, hilarity burst out as someone hit the punch line of a joke.

No air kisses, no networking, no maneuvering to get close to the photographer.

It was, quite possibly, the happiest party Damon had ever seen. No, it wasn't hip and full of famous or almost-famous people. It was simply full of people who were having fun.

But he wasn't there as a guest, he was there to work. Skirting the room unobtrusively, he searched for Cady. He wanted to find her to discuss scheduling. He needed to find her, because it had been too damned long since he'd held her, soft and sweet, in his arms.

He rounded the DJ's booth, scanning the faces, looking for the red of her hair. And when he saw it, he felt his heart stop. After a moment, it started beating again, but fast and hard this time, as though caged in his chest. It was Cady before him, but looking as he'd never seen her before. He'd thought she'd looked dressed up at the restaurant in her prim tuxedo, but he'd had no idea.

She wore a dress of some silky material that swished and flowed in sea blues and the vivid greens of the ferns that grew around the pines, and every shade in between. It swirled around her calves and dipped low over her breasts. She'd darkened her eyes and done something to her mouth that temporarily unhinged his thought processes. Her hair looked softer, shinier, more richly red.

It was more than that, though. There was a glow to her as though she was lit from within. And she was standing next to some guy, standing next to him and laughing, even when he put his arm around her waist and leaned over to kiss her.

Damon's jaw tightened. He'd never been a jealous guy. There was no reason to be now.

So why did he feel as if he could chew nails?

Consciously, he made himself relax and crossed to her. "Cady."

She whirled around and the smile broke over her face like sunlight. And everything was right again in his world. "Oh, Damon, hi."

"Hi. How's the party going?"

"Everything's great." The words were rapid, her voice breathless. "Tell Roman and the guys in the kitchen they rock."

"I'll do that."

"And you rock, too." Mischief flickered in her eyes. "I want you to meet a couple of people. This is my brother, Walker." She nodded to the dark-haired guy. "Walker, this is Damon Hurst, the chef."

He could see the resemblance now, something in the mouth, the set of the eyes. And he relaxed, putting out his hand with real pleasure. "Good to meet you."

"This is great," Walker said. "My wife and I were huge fans of Pommes de Terre."

"You live in Manhattan?"

Walker nodded. "We went to Pommes all the time. I was addicted to the sweetbreads. I don't suppose you're doing them up here, are you?"

"Not so far," Damon said, trying to focus on the conversation when all he wanted to do was get Cady to himself and just inhale her.

Walker shook his head. "Too bad. My mom tells me I don't visit enough. If you had sweetbreads on the menu, I'd be up all the time."

"What are sweetbreads?" Cady asked.

"Never mind," Damon said. "You don't want to know."

"How will I be able to avoid them if I don't know what they are or what they look like?"

"I guess you'll just have to trust me."

She shot him a suspicious look. "This isn't like the squid brain thing, is it?"

"Wait and find out."

It was as though for an instant they were enclosed in their own private bubble where all that mattered was the connection between them. Neither of them noticed the sharp glance Walker gave Damon.

The tall, thin brunette standing next to Cady cleared her throat.

"Oh, right. Sorry." Cady shook her head. "Damon, meet my good friend Tania. She's a big fan of yours."

He shook her hand. "The reader," he said. "Hair scrunchies."

"Hair scrunchies?" Tania repeated in confusion while Cady blushed furiously.

"Nice to meet you," he said. "I need to borrow Cady for a minute."

He drew her over to the waiting area, around the corner to

the maître d's desk. He ached to lose himself in the heat of her mouth, the soft press of her body, that apple scent that just about drove him around the bend. He ached to bury himself in her. Instead, he drew her hands to his mouth and pressed his lips to them.

"You're beautiful," he said.

She stared at him, eyes wide. He practically saw her decide not to take him seriously. "Flattery will get you everywhere."

"It's not flattery. I'd prove it but I figure you'd say it's not the time or the place."

"That old problem again." There was high color in her cheeks so that she looked lit from within. "Do you think we might arrange a time and place?"

"I think when the party's over we might just be able to do that," he told her. "Speaking of which, how much longer do you want happy hour to go? We need to know when to start plating soups and salads."

She pondered. "I suppose the faster dinner gets going, the sooner we get to that time and place, right?"

"Probably."

"Well—" she glanced at her watch "—how about another fifteen minutes of cocktail hour and then I'll get people sitting down?"

He glanced at his watch. "Seven o'clock, then?"

"Seven o'clock it is."

"I'll do my best to have them cutting the cake by seven-fifteen," he said. As she laughed, he couldn't keep himself from leaning in just to taste her for a moment. "And after, I'll see you."

Even the party to end all parties had to wind down sometime. The cake had long since been demolished, the echoes of the toasts faded, when people began kissing good-night and trailing out the door in small groups.

With every departure, Cady felt her pulse beat harder. With

every departure, she felt more certain. She and Max walked her parents back to their house and kissed them good-night. When Max opened her car door to get in, Cady rummaged in her pocket.

"What are these for?" Max blinked at the keys Cady handed her.

"So you can get in."

"How are you going to get home?" Max looked her up and down. "Or do I even need to ask?"

Cady let out some of the laughter that had been bubbling through her all night. "I think I can find a ride." She hardly felt she needed one. Somehow, she felt that if she took a deep breath she'd just float off the ground and over to Damon's.

"I guess the dress was a success."

"I guess it was. Will you be okay on your own tonight?"

Max leaned in and kissed her cheek. "I think I can figure out how to work your DVD player. Be good."

"I'll be great," Cady said.

And so it was that she was waiting when Damon stepped out of the restaurant, last of all the kitchen help.

"Hey." She stepped out of the shadows.

"Hey, yourself."

"Can I hitch a ride?"

"I'll take you anywhere you want to go," he said.

And on this night, of all nights, it seemed anything was possible.

A full moon hung above them, silvering everything, making it dreamlike and magical as they wound through wood and field to his house. There was so much to say but they turned, instead, to touch. A stroke of a hand on bare skin, a touch of lips. They kissed when they stood at the front door and they kissed again inside, with moonlight shining through every window. And they kissed in his bedroom as the silver light streamed in from above.

There were words but no need for them as they stood together. Damon trailed his fingertips up her sides almost worshipfully, barely touching, making her shiver. Beautiful, he'd said, and for the first time in her life, she felt it. The back of her dress parted as he unfastened it, and it whispered down her body to fall in a ring at her feet. She felt him trail its path with lips and tongue. Beautiful, he'd said, and as he gazed at her, she saw it in his eyes.

Her fingers slipped through his hair, stroked his cheek as he lifted her and carried her to the bed. When he came to lie beside her, the warmth of his naked skin against hers was a benediction. And the joy just burst through her.

Pleasure led to pleasure as they sank into each other, savoring taste, savoring touch. Each caress was a treasure, each response a gift. When he poised himself over her body, she found herself breathless. Gaze locked on hers, he slid inside. His strokes were slow and deliberate. With every movement she felt as though they were connected by something beyond a physical link.

This was more than sex, she realized in wonder. This was something she'd never felt before. What usually flamed fast and furious now burned slow and deep, the naked flame becoming the smoldering coal that glowed and ultimately consumed. They were borne along by more than physical sensation. This wasn't arousal, it was emotion incarnate.

When their bodies quickened to the point of inevitability, they cried out together. When she felt the climax rush through her, she tasted her tears. After, in the spill of moonlight, he gathered her to him.

And in the spill of moonlight, she knew at last—she was in love with him.

Chapter Sixteen

You could always tell where you were in the growing season by how far you had to park from the farmers' market, Cady reflected as she walked in. And by how many people you had to dodge. There were easily twice the number of booths in the market now as there had been when she'd visited with Damon two months before—not to mention twice the number of bodies. If she hadn't known better, she'd have sworn it wasn't the same place, so much had changed.

Then again, so much had changed about her life, period. When she'd walked these rows with Damon, she'd never have guessed she'd wind up even talking to him voluntarily, let alone having an affair with him. And she never in a million years would have dreamed that she'd go and fall in love with him. The Cady she'd been then would have not-so-diplomatically suggested she have her head examined.

The Cady of today wasn't so sure that was a bad idea.

It would be okay, she told herself even as her stomach jittered. No, falling in love with him wouldn't have been her choice, but it wasn't as though she could tell herself not to feel. After all, she'd already tried that, for all the good it had done her. At heart, Cady was a realist, and her heart, it seemed, would do as it would.

She remembered waking that morning, surfacing from sleep to warmth and sunlight and the feel of Damon's arms around her. Yes, loving him was a risk with an uncertain ending, but wasn't it worth it, just once in her life to feel so treasured and cared for? Wasn't it worth it to have that feeling she'd always dreamed of?

"Hey, Cady!"

She headed into Pete Tebeau's booth. "Hey, Pete, how are you?"

"If I was any better I'd get arrested." He winked as he weighed tomatoes for a customer. "And how about you? Whatever it is you're taking, I want some."

"Just clean living, Pete." She grinned. It was becoming something of a habit, she realized.

"What brings you down here? I'd gotten used to seeing Hizzoner. Didn't think I was ever gonna see you again."

"Damon's got a photo shoot for some big food magazine today. They're interviewing him and everything. I volunteered to come here."

"Lucky me," he said, finishing with the customer and turning to her. "What's that you've got there?"

Cady glanced down at the tray in her hands. Nothing ventured, nothing gained, she told herself. "That's the other reason I came up. I've got a proposition for you, Pete."

He winked. "Definitely lucky me."

"I'm trying to be serious," she scolded.

"So am I. What are those guys, sprouts?"

"Microgreens. Damon uses them on all of his dishes. A lot of chefs do, apparently, but they're not easy to get. He seems to think that there might be a local market for them." She took a breath. "What do you think about putting them out here and seeing if anybody buys them? If they do, I'll give you a piece of the take."

He considered. "I can't see people getting too wild over grass but they eat alfalfa sprouts, so what do I know? And Damon was right about those ramps," he added. "I can't see the harm in trying. How much do you want for them?"

When she told him, he whistled. "You really think they'll pay that?"

"Believe it or not, that's less than the going rate. And they're local."

He shrugged. "Well, set 'em down there. We'll see what happens."

There was little Damon disliked as much as a photo shoot. Over the course of his career, he'd come to regard it as a necessary evil but one only tolerated, at best. Sure, he'd spent years on camera during his Cooking Channel tenure, but that had always been in the context of doing. Either he was joking and chatting up the live audience of his show or he was in competition, focusing on his cuisine.

With the photo shoots, it was just him and the camera. He wasn't sure which he liked least, posing or going about the business of cooking while pretending that he wasn't aware of the lens following his every move.

And Francesca watching him from across the room.

Finally, though, it was done. The photographer moved to shoot the restaurant and he and Francesca moved to the dining room.

"All right," she said, "now feed me."

They sat at a table covered with tasting plates and he watched her sample her way through the menu with concentration but surprisingly little enjoyment. He couldn't help remembering the pleasure on Cady's face the day he'd fed her the *croustillant*. For Francesca, it was an intellectual exercise; for Cady, it was a journey of the senses.

With her fork, Francesca prodded the bread of an appetizer. "You're doing lobster rolls now?"

"When in Maine," he said.

She picked out a miniscule bite and nibbled. "Lobster, parsley, aioli," she said thoughtfully, "and…"

"Lobster."

"That's all?" She frowned. "What was all this about re-imagining the classics?"

"You've been eating it." He nodded at the other dishes.

"I'm not eating it right now."

"Some things don't need to be reimagined. Some things are good just as they are."

She flicked a glance at the ceiling. "You're not on that tiresome 'less is more' rant again, are you?"

She was a food editor. Food was supposed to matter. "I'm not on any rant," he said. "I'm just cooking."

"I see. Well, you cooked, I ate, I'm stuffed. Why don't we go outside and walk so I can work off some of it?" She rose.

"You won't have to walk far." Damon glanced at the nearly untouched plates. "I can't say I saw you take a full bite of anything."

"You chefs are always so sensitive. If I really ate everywhere I went, I'd be enormous."

"Now who's talking about less is more?"

She patted her flat stomach. "You men have it easy with your metabolisms. Some of us have to work at it."

Why, he wondered, would a person choose a job in food if they didn't like eating? He followed her out the door, but it was Cady he thought of. Whether it was a burger or the Dover sole he'd made her a few days before, she always ate the way she made love, with pleasure and abandon.

"How wonderfully picturesque," Francesca pronounced as they walked toward the water. "Not just boats but a gazebo, too. It's so quaint, I can't stand it."

He couldn't have said why her comment annoyed him. "It's just Grace Harbor."

"Someplace has to be, I suppose. So?" She flicked him an expectant glance. "Talk to me."

"About what?"

"Anything." She stepped into the gazebo, her heels thunking on the wood floor. "Competing chefs, your take on the current state of American cuisine, what the enfant terrible of American cuisine is doing next."

Damon looked pained. "Can we stop already with the enfant terrible bit? I haven't been an *enfant* for a few decades now."

"Oh, but it makes such good copy, darling. Otherwise, what else will I write about?"

"It's a food magazine. You could write about the food."

She settled herself on the gazebo's bench. "There's only so much I can gush about your cooking, as exquisite as it is. And it is exquisite. Much as it pains me to admit it, that tenderloin was nothing short of divine."

"Watch out, Francesca, you're going to turn my head." Folding his arms, he leaned against a nearby pillar.

"At least tell me about being a tortured genius and clawing your way back from obscurity. Because this cover story will put you back on top, you know. You'll owe me."

She said it lightly but something told him it wasn't a joke to her. There was nothing Francesca liked better than being in control.

"Have you at least kicked a customer out lately?" she continued. "It's rather like a christening for you, isn't it? Instead of breaking champagne on the doorway of a new restaurant, you toss a customer in the parking lot."

"I've been learning restraint in my old age."

"I hope you haven't gotten too restrained. That can be terribly boring, you know." She draped an arm over the railing. "You were always one of the ones I relied on for a bit of entertainment."

"I was one of the ones you relied on for a punch line."

"Not to mention other things," she said, eyeing him appraisingly. "Country life seems to agree with you. It must be the air around here. Everyone is so marvelously robust." She glanced over to where Cady stood on a ladder, trimming dead flowers off the rhododendrons.

Damon gave a faint frown. He would have used many words to describe Cady, but robust wouldn't have been among them.

"Speaking of robust, I'm staying overnight before I drive home. I'll be depending on you to keep the evening from becoming a total loss."

"Francesca, we'll be doing a hundred and twelve covers tonight. At least. You're welcome to have dinner but I'll be in the kitchen."

She looked at him from under her lashes. "I was talking about after service, darling."

"This is a small town. They roll up the streets at midnight."

She put a hand on his arm. "Then I guess we'll have to make our own fun."

It was about this time of year that the warm weather didn't seem quite so pleasant. Cady stood on the ladder and swiped her hair back off her forehead. Hot, sticky, tiring. And of course seeing Damon with his glamorous magazine editor somehow made it all worse.

She'd watched them walk out to the gazebo together, the woman in a white blouse with the sleeves rolled up and a narrow leather skirt with some sort of wide, pewter-colored belt. She had wavy blond hair put up in one of those tousled, effortlessly sexy knots that probably took hours to get right. Her chunky jewelry somehow only made her look more feminine.

Cady felt her T-shirt sticking to her back.

It was a different life, she thought, clipping a faded bloom from the rhodie. And even though she despised herself for it, she couldn't help wondering if Damon found the reporter woman attractive. Cady hoped to God not, because if that truly was the kind of look he went for, he was with the wrong woman.

Or she was the wrong woman for him.

He'd called her beautiful, Cady reminded herself. Of course, that had been when she'd been dressed up within an inch of her life. It wasn't the day-to-day her. But it was the day-to-day her that he kept coming back to. That was something to hold on to, wasn't it?

She climbed back down the ladder to gather the dead heads she'd discarded into a waste bag. From over at the gazebo, she heard a low, throaty laugh. An intimate laugh. None of her business, she told herself, folding up the ladder. It was just Damon doing his job, as she was doing hers. But she couldn't help glancing over before she walked away.

They were in the gazebo, Damon at the entrance, the woman just inside. She gave that laugh again and touched his forearm and suddenly Cady knew.

He'd slept with her.

She could feel the rush of blood to her face. Paranoia, she told herself as she hurried away toward the toolshed. There was no way she could look at them and know. But there was something in the lines of their bodies, something in the way the woman looked up at him. And for all that Cady tried to tell herself she was crazy, down in her bones she knew—it may not have been recent, it may not have been often, but they'd made love.

And now she was back, just like his old life was back.

Why the hell hadn't he seen it coming? Damon wondered in frustration. He knew how Francesca worked, he should have been paying more attention. Instead, he'd let himself get distracted by Cady. If he'd been concentrating, he could have turned the discussion, packed Francesca off to her hotel with a wave and a smile. Of course, it was too late for that now—the offer was out on the table.

Subtlety had never been Francesca's strong suit. Their only liaison had happened after a charity dinner at which he'd been one of the celebrity chefs. They'd fallen into bed for a bout of gymnastic sex that had exhausted his interest long before it had exhausted her. He'd never felt any urge for a rematch.

Apparently, that made one of them.

"I'm in guesthouse two, on the top floor," she said now, the invitation ripe in her eyes and in her voice.

And he damned well needed to find a diplomatic way to turn it down.

He shook his head. "I've got a long day in the kitchen, Francesca. I don't do the all-night party thing anymore. I like to be awake when I'm using sharp knives."

"What are you doing working lunch and dinner? Don't you have line cooks for that?"

"Yes, and I'm one of them."

She raised a brow. "This isn't the Damon Hurst we all know and love."

"Right. Look, we should finish up. I've got to get back in to start lunch service." And he hoped to God she'd take the face-saving out.

Instead, she smiled and stroked his forearm with her finger. "You know what they say about all work and no play. I think we need to do something about that."

He jerked his arm away. "No, all right?"

She stared. "Excuse me?"

"Francesca." He let out a breath. "Look, I appreciate you

coming up, I appreciate the story. It was good to see you, but let's leave it at that."

For an instant, the look in her eyes was absolutely murderous. An instant later, it was masked so completely that he couldn't be sure he'd seen it. "You always take things so seriously." Her voice was chill. "I was only joking. We're leaving tomorrow at an ungodly hour."

"I'll walk you to your guesthouse."

"Don't bother." Just for an instant, the anger flashed, then it was gone. "After all, you've got lunch service."

Perfect, Damon thought as she stalked away. Now she was ticked at him and it was anybody's guess what would happen to his cover story. Probably a nice little visit to the round file. There had to have been a better way to handle it.

It didn't make him any less irritated with himself to realize that none of it would have happened if he'd never been stupid enough to sleep with her in the first place. Of course, he could as easily kick himself for playing the field or for deciding to become a chef in the first place.

He sighed. What was done was done. With luck, Francesca would cool down and find the humor in it and everything would be okay. And he went back to the restaurant, trying to ignore the little knot of uneasiness in his gut.

It wound up being easier than he'd expected, courtesy of a couple of runners who collided during the lunch rush, sending food flying into the lane between stoves and counter. There wasn't time in the middle of firing orders to clear the line, so they let Denny mop around them, a mistake Damon recognized only after Rosalie slipped on a missed bit of sautéed pearl onion and fell to sprain her wrist.

He'd never expected to see the day when he was sorry that the restaurant was now packed the better part of the time. They always had to work fast. Being minus a cook, though, meant working at the speed of light, without letup until close. Even if he had planned a liaison with Francesca at the end of the night, Damon reflected sardonically, he wouldn't have had the energy for it. He barely had time to look up, let alone stop.

Or find any time to see Cady. But he couldn't keep himself from stealing a couple of minutes during a lag in dinner service to give her a quick call.

"Hello?"

Just hearing her voice gave him more energy. "Hey," he said as the nearby printer chattered. "I hope your day's going better than mine."

"It's been all right." She sounded remote, tired.

"Sorry I didn't get over to say hello today. We kind of had a disaster here. Rosalie got hurt and we've been in the weeds ever since."

"I'm sorry to hear that." She paused. "How did your interview go?"

He thought a minute. He'd probably be smart to tell her about Francesca but not while he was standing in the kitchen with an audience. "It was…interesting, I guess you could say."

"Interesting?"

"In a manner of speaking. I'll give you the scoop later. Maybe tonight after I get off? Although I can't guarantee I'll be of much use."

"Why don't you just stay at your place? You'll get more sleep that way."

It made sense on the face of it, but somehow it felt like being pushed away. "All right." He frowned. "Hey, are you feeling all right? You sound a little off."

"Rough afternoon, same as you. I left early."

"Well, get some sleep. You can tell me about it tomorrow. We'll definitely make some time to get together."

"Sure," she said, "we'll do that."

And he disconnected, feeling distant from her in some indefinable way.

* * *

The snatch of music from his cell phone dragged him up out of sleep at dawn. He woke sprawled out across the bed. A bed he'd been in too short a time. Blinking groggily, he fumbled for his handset as it rang again.

"'Lo," he mumbled.

"We've got a problem."

Damon rubbed his eyes. "Jack?"

"Yeah, it's Jack. What the hell did you say to Francesca?"

"Huh?" He fought to get some of the cobwebs out of his brain. "Francesca? What are you talking about?"

"What did you tell her?"

"Let me wake up here, for chrissakes."

There was a pause. "You haven't seen, then."

"No, whatever it is, I haven't. We got slammed last night. I didn't get home until late." His alarm started to chirp and he jabbed it. Six o'clock, he saw. Joy. "All right, what's the deal?"

"Her blog."

The back of Damon's neck began to prickle. He vaguely remembered hearing something about a blog six or eight months before, but by then he'd been too far into his own free fall to care. "What does it say?"

"Start up your computer and read it for yourself."

He rose to go into his home office. It gave him time to become fully awake. At the Web site, he watched a photo of Francesca unfurl on the page. And was it just his imagination or was there something subtly predatory about her smile?

Her blog was a combination of industry gossip, reviews and sneak peeks of what was ahead in the magazine.

The problem was, one of those peeks was him.

…Meanwhile, Damon Hurst is up to his old tricks. When *Dining Well* visited him at his new Maine restaurant, the food was, as always, exquisite. But then, the food never was Hurst's problem, at least when he could be bothered to stop by the kitchen. Here, he does a splendid job of reinventing New England favorites. Too bad he's not so good at reinventing himself. Both service and execution at the actual restaurant were reminiscent of the bad old days at the end of his Pommes de Terre tenure. It appears that Damon Hurst may have finally won the crown as this generation's chef who failed to live up to his promise. Look for more details in our upcoming issue of *Dining Well*.

"Well?" Jack said.

"Jesus."

"That's one way of putting it."

"I told you we were slammed last night. We were minus a cook. Maybe she got a bad meal." That wasn't what it was about, though, and he knew it.

"What does she know that I don't know, Damon? What have you been up to?"

"Nothing. It wasn't about what I did." Damon rubbed his temples. "It was about what I didn't do. After service."

There was a short silence. "Ah."

"Yeah, ah."

"The lady doesn't take rejection well."

"Who does?"

"In this case, she can do a lot of damage." Jack blew out a breath. "You're lucky I know Francesca. Plenty of people don't, people in a position to make decisions."

"Like your friend Stephanopolous?"

"Like him. He's not going to follow a food blog, but I guarantee you he's got a clipping service or a couple of bright boys who keep an eye on the press. She's going to try to bury you with that article. It could be a problem."

"Weren't you telling me you had complete control?"

"The man believes in delegating, not giving the store away. The minute he hears that you're a discipline problem, you'll be history. If you want in on this deal, you need to have a track record with him before Francesca's little hatchet job sees the light of day. Are you in or out?"

In or out. "I can't just give you an answer, Jack. I've got to at least see the place."

"Do you not get the scope of this operation? The place isn't an issue. You don't like the kitchen? We redo it. Problems with the dining room? We bring in a designer. As long as we're making money within six months, he won't care. And we can do that if we've got you in place and branded."

Damon stared at Francesca's smirk. Everything he ever wanted.

Except Cady.

"I need to think about it."

"Well, guess what? This fiasco with Francesca just took away that option. You've got to decide now. We've got two months, max, to get our own PR spin in place before her issue hits the newsstands."

"The best defense is a good offense?"

"The best defense is making money. This is a big job, Damon. And you're the right guy for it, no doubt. But the window's closing. And if you're in, I need you here tomorrow."

"I'm not going to take a job sight unseen, Jack." Even if he had done just that with the Sextant, a sneaky voice in his head reminded him.

"Fine," Jack snapped. "Call it an interview, if you want. There'll be a ticket waiting for you at the airport in Portland. Just get your butt on that plane."

Part of him couldn't understand why he was hesitating. Part of him couldn't understand how he could possibly go. The stakes were huge and there was no right choice. There was only the path of least regret.

"Come on," Jack urged, "isn't this what you've been waiting for, the right opportunity? It doesn't get any more right than this, buddy. Think about it, restaurants in Tokyo, Dubai, London. It's what we always talked about, only bigger. We can do everything we've ever wanted to, everything we've ever thought of. So tell me, are you in or are you out?"

Damon hesitated.

"Are you in or out?"

Grace Harbor…Vegas…Stephanopolous…the Compass Rose…the Sextant…an empire…Cady…

The world.

He swallowed. "I'm in," he said.

He caught up with her in the greenhouse. She looked tired, he saw when he leaned in to kiss her, as though she hadn't slept well.

"Hey," he said and closed the door behind him. "Got a couple of minutes? I need to talk to you."

It would be okay, he told himself when she nodded. They could make this work. They would make this work.

He took a breath. "You remember my buddy Jack Worth? The guy you met last week?"

"The ex-partner, right?" She kept working, stacking plants together in carrier trays on a table by the door.

"Yeah. The thing is, he wasn't just stopping by. He came to talk to me about a job."

Her hands stilled.

"There's a casino in Las Vegas put up by Dimitri Stephanopolous, the biggest one in town. He's dumped a bundle into it. They're having problems with the restaurants, though, and they've brought Jack in to manage them." Damon paused. There was no easy way to say it. "He wants me to be the executive chef."

It was like having all the breath punched out of her. Whatever she'd expected, it wasn't that. "Las Vegas?" Cady echoed. "What did you tell him?"

He didn't answer right away. "I agreed to come out," he said finally. "I want to see the place, meet the people. After that, we'll see."

He hadn't even bothered to visit the Compass Rose before taking the job at the Sextant. Because he'd known all along that it didn't matter—he was going to leave. Anger set her blood simmering. Without thinking about it, she started to pace.

"Cady, it's a great opportunity."

"Funny, I thought this was supposed to be the big opportunity. Whatever happened to the line you fed my parents about building something here? Of course, Grace Harbor can hardly compete with Vegas." And she couldn't compete with any of it.

"You don't understand. The Stephanopolous operation, it's a lot more than just the casino. He's one of the biggest developers in the world. We do this right, the sky is the limit." He shook his head. "I can't turn this down. I have to at least look."

Her jaw felt stiff. "You're not looking. You've already decided."

Now it was his turn to get angry. "I'm just talking to them, that's all. I just wanted to tell you. And your parents."

"Why, so they can have a day's notice? Dammit, Damon, it's not fair," she burst out, whirling toward him. "They *trusted* you. They gave you a chance. They thought you meant it when you said you wanted to stay."

"I did mean it. I never expected this."

"Oh darn, tough times for you, huh? And you can walk out without looking back because you never even bothered to sign a contract."

"Your parents didn't want one."

"That's because they're the kind of people who keep their word without paper."

"And I keep mine," he shot back. "Look, I don't know why we're arguing. There's a way to make this work. I've already talked to Jack about it. If I do take the Vegas job, I need to start as soon as possible but one week out of the month I'll be out here. That means I can work with Roman until your parents find a new executive chef. And that means we can see each other."

She stared at him. "See each other?"

"Cady, whatever else is going on, this thing between us is important to me. I don't want to lose it. I want to find a way to make it work."

"Are you out of your mind? There is no us. You're walking out on my parents. You're walking out on me."

Temper flashed in his eyes. "I'm not walking out."

"You think for one minute that you're going to be coming back once you get out there? You're lying to yourself. Vegas, the casinos, the nonstop party people," she flared. "It's all right up your alley." And it hurt, oh, it hurt.

"So we're back to this again, all the stories? Haven't you seen anything while I've been here? Don't you know me? That's not my life anymore."

"And this is? Who are you trying to kid? This was never your thing. Grace Harbor was never your kind of thing. It was just a convenient fill-in so you could keep your chops sharp. And I suppose I was, too. I'm such an *idiot*." Her voice rose. "I knew from the beginning what you were like, I *knew* it, and I still got suckered." And it cut deep, slicing her to the bone. She'd let him in, she'd trusted, she'd given up that last bit of distance, that last bit of protection.

And she'd given up her heart.

"You were never a fill-in," he shot back. "You matter. This matters."

She couldn't let herself listen. "If it matters, then why are you leaving?"

"Don't you see, Cady? I've been waiting for this kind of thing my whole life. There's no limit to where I can take it. I shouldn't even be debating, but I am. Because I look at you and me and I don't know if there's a limit there, either."

"Stop it," she flung at him. "It's just lines, like everything else you've said. You're standing here saying all the pretty things and you've already got both feet back in your old life." Her throat ached. "God, Damon, look around. It's all coming back, your groupies, your photo shoots, your ex-partner. Your ex-lover."

The words hung in the air.

"Francesca." Damon shook his head "I don't know what you saw but there's nothing going on there."

"She's just your type, just like Vegas is just your life."

"It was one night, a long time ago."

"Dammit, Damon, I don't care," Cady returned passionately. "It doesn't matter, don't you see? She's not the problem, she's just a symptom. Who she is, what she represents, that's your world, not mine. It's not Grace Harbor, it's not anything we can be. So just go, grab your brass ring. It's what you've always wanted. Take it and be happy." She turned away because she was very afraid she was going to weep.

She heard him step up behind her. "You've got it all figured out, don't you?" he said quietly. "There's really nothing I can say, nothing I can do except go and let you just have the rest of this conversation with yourself." He lifted his hands. "That's all you're doing anyway."

"And what about you?" she whispered.

"Oh yeah, I forgot. You know all about me. Except you don't know me at all." He hesitated. "Goodbye, Cady."

She heard the door close and heard his feet crunch on the gravel. And she slid down to the floor and curled into a ball.

Chapter Seventeen

Cady hated crying, she always had. Even when she'd fallen off her bike as a child and skinned her knee, she'd always done everything she possibly could not to cry. It hurt. It made her feel weak, powerless. It made her feel as if she'd given in.

And when it was over, she felt empty.

This time, though, there was no choice. She couldn't hold it back. Damon had told her once that the right relationship could change her world. It had. It had brought her pleasure, laughter and immense joy. It had brought her pain, betrayal, anguish and, finally, loss.

And so she cried, letting the sobs rack her body until she emptied herself. Because even emptiness was better than heartache.

It was later, she couldn't have said how long, that the door opened again. This time, it was her mother's voice that she heard.

"Honey?"

Cady got up hastily, swiping at her cheeks. "Don't say it," she warned. *And don't be nice. Oh, please, don't be nice.*

Amanda shook her head gently. "I'm not going to say anything. I was just coming to see if you were all right."

"I'm fine." She squared her shoulders. "You heard the news, I take it."

"I did."

"Is he gone?" she asked, even as she despised herself for it.

"Yes, he's gone."

The unbearable truth. "If you had a contract, you could sue him." She paced away and turned. Easier to focus on the anger, to put up a wall against all the other emotions that crowded around. Easier that, than to feel.

"We don't want to sue him," Amanda said. "I might want to skin him alive for messing with my daughter, but there's no reason to sue him, even if we could. We took our chances, we got something out of it. Sure, we'd rather have had him for a year or two, but we still got the press." She was quiet a moment. "But you know I'd have given all of that up to keep you from being hurt."

Cady's throat ached again. "I'm okay," she said.

"No, you're not."

"All right, maybe I'm not. But I'll get over it."

"If it's any comfort, we told him to just go. He won't be back."

He won't be back.

It wasn't any comfort, Cady thought. It wasn't any comfort at all.

And blindly, she turned into her mother's arms.

He drank scotch and looked out the window of the plane to the solid mass of cloud cover below. It had always bothered him, flying over featureless white that gave no clue as to what lay beneath. He didn't like not knowing where he was. It was disorienting.

Then again, there was something pretty damned disorienting about knowing that his life had gone to hell in a handbasket even as he found himself flying out to accept the opportunity of a lifetime. He should have been happy.

He shouldn't have been feeling as though his guts had been kicked in.

He didn't know what was worse, having Cady tell him to take a hike or realizing that she hadn't ever really known him at all. That she'd never trusted him. That the world he thought they'd built between them was nothing.

In a way, she'd made his decision easier. Once she'd taken herself out of the picture, the choice was simple. There really was nothing to lose.

The Sextant was strictly a short-term assignment, had been from the beginning. Certainly Ian McBain had shown little surprise at the news. "We had you longer than we expected, to be honest," he'd said.

There had been something in Amanda McBain's eyes as she'd looked at him that made Damon suspect she knew about him and Cady. When she told him he didn't need to worry about notice, he was certain of it.

And Cady… It had been a hell of a way to say goodbye. But maybe there wasn't any good way. And maybe she was right, maybe it had been an impossible situation from the start. But what was he supposed to do, throw a career away, jettison everything he'd worked for to stay in Grace Harbor, work at the Sextant, live on the small stage?

It wasn't possible and she should have known it. And it hadn't had to be the end of them. They could have kept things going, with him flying out, her coming to Vegas. They could have found a way if she'd been willing to try. If she'd been willing to trust him. But she hadn't.

And that had hurt worst of all.

And so he sat in business class drinking scotch, watching the clouds pass below. And wishing he knew where the hell he was.

There was nothing like having your life turned upside down to make you focus on work, Cady discovered over the next week. She dug and raked, hauled and swept, tore out flower beds, rolled and reseeded lawns, anything to exhaust herself. She took on any project she could, manicured the Compass Rose to within an inch of its life. She welcomed the approach of the solstice as the days grew ever longer, giving her fewer and fewer hours to be trapped inside with nothing to do but think.

Because thinking was the impossible part.

So she kept her music player turned up to full volume, loud enough to distract herself. And as one day bled into the next, she avoided the greenhouse with its memories.

She was aerating the back lawn of the Compass Rose when the phone in her pocket vibrated. She stopped and took off her headphones. "Hello?"

"Hey, Cady, where are you?" Pete Tebeau bawled out of the receiver.

"Hi, Pete. I'm working."

"I haven't seen any of you guys in a week. What's up?"

"Damon's not around. I haven't had time to stop by." And hadn't been able to bear to.

"Well, aren't you going to come get your money?"

"For what?"

"The grass."

"Grass," she repeated, before her thought processes kicked in. The microgreens, of course. The microgreens she hadn't checked in almost a week.

"Oh, hell, I completely forgot. Did they sell?"

"Like hotcakes. And now I got a whole crowd of folks sloping around here waiting for more. I was hoping you were bringing some."

"I can't do it today," she told him, glancing at her watch. By the time she hit Portland, the market would be winding down, and anyway, she had no idea if she even had anything to sell. The microgreens from the week before were probably well on their way to being macrogreens. She'd need to plant more.

"What do you want me to tell 'em?"

"Tell them…" She thought for a minute. "Tell them to check back in two weeks. I'll have more then and we can set up a regular supply if they want them."

"Regular, huh? If you're going to do that, you better get yourself a booth."

She just couldn't think about it for now. "Can't I sell them through you, at least temporarily?"

"You know where to find me," he said. "Hey, when's Damon gonna be back? I got some of them heirloom tomatoes he asked me to plant coming on."

"He's not coming back," she said, struggling to keep her voice toneless.

"At all?"

"No. He's gone for good." Gone for good.

She didn't think she could bear it.

At the back of the property, the greenhouse glowed white. Since the day Damon had left, she'd stayed away. The last thing she wanted to do was step back inside and into the tangle of memories. But the reprieve, she'd known, was only temporary. Sooner or later, she was going to have to go tend to the plants inside.

And that time, it appeared, was now.

She'd known all along it was going to end, she reminded herself. She knew that nobody changed down deep. She wasn't going to remember the days he'd kissed her here. She wasn't going to remember how he'd made her laugh. And she wasn't going to remember the way he'd made her ache at the end.

So she turned up her music player as loud as it would go, and listened to Lucinda Williams sing about changing the locks as she stepped through the door.

It was all right, was her first relieved thought. She could handle it. Sure, memories of Damon lurked everywhere but she could put them aside and take care of business. Life would go on. She'd survive. And maybe someday the bad memories would fade enough to allow her to savor the good.

For now, she was just happy to see that the plants looked okay. Perhaps a few out of reach of the full stream of the automatic sprayers were a bit droopy but it was nothing that a good watering wouldn't cure.

She turned on her hose and moved along the tables, spraying the plants that needed it. It wasn't until she reached her workbench that she saw the microgreens.

Or what remained of them.

She'd forgotten, she thought as she stared, stricken. They'd been on her workbench, not on one of the tables with the sprayers. They hadn't gotten water in a week. She remembered how they'd looked before, vibrant and green and cared for. Now, they looked as if they'd been put under one of the kitchen's salamanders, withered to limp brown strings.

They'd struggled to stay alive but they were delicate, more than she'd realized. They couldn't survive neglect. They couldn't take being abandoned. They couldn't take being left behind.

She felt her throat tighten, as it had done so many times over the past week. Left behind, just as she had been. He'd gone without a backward glance, just packed his clothes, locked his door and—

His door. His house. Good Lord, she thought suddenly, his garden. A week had gone by, a week without rain or water for the delicate seedlings. Dozens of plants, all of them dependent on care. All of them needing attention to survive.

She turned for the door. The two of them had worked together to put the garden in. And maybe Damon was gone and maybe what was between them had withered, but she couldn't let living things suffer for it.

She couldn't see what they'd planted together die.

The office was the size of the entire kitchen at the Sextant. Then again, the kitchen at Pommes de Terre Vegas was probably the size of the entire restaurant in Maine, Damon thought. And the dining room, well, even during his headiest days in Manhattan he couldn't have imagined turning out four hundred and fifty dinners a night.

Of course, he wasn't turning them out, that was part of the problem. He had a staff of more than two dozen cooks, including a sous chef and a head chef over him to manage them all. And that was only in the flagship restaurant. Damon's job was to wander through the kitchens a couple of nights a week, taste a soup here, inspect a plate there, and…

Go quietly nuts.

He'd made over the menus his first week on the job, netted a series of reviews gushing about the extraordinary cuisine during the second. By the third week, he was on the press tour, starting with the papers and travel journals and moving up to morning shows around the country.

In the flood of positive press, Francesca's malicious blog had sunk without a trace. The actual magazine had yet to come out, but it hardly mattered now. Three of the four restaurants were operating in the black, which was the only thing that really counted.

At least he tried to tell himself that.

The real issue was that now that the initial rush of activity was over, he was at loose ends. Oh, there was a deal in the works for another cookbook, but outside of working up the odd special and making one of his periodic inspections, he was left with far too much time on his hands.

He'd spent the final three or four years of his time in Manhattan letting others do the cooking. It hadn't bothered him because he'd been so busy with television and book tours and parties that the kitchen had turned into an obligation. But the time he'd spent on the line at the Sextant had reminded him of why he'd chosen the profession in the first place, the time he'd spent dreaming up new dishes, the time he'd spent teaching Roman.

The time he'd spent cooking for Cady.

He cut off that line of thought immediately. He wasn't going to let himself wonder about her. He wasn't going to remember her apple-cinnamon scent or how it felt to wake with her in the morning. Instead, he rose and walked down to the kitchen. To hell with his staff of twenty-four. A couple of hours of working the line during the Saturday dinner rush ought to take care of the funk he was in.

It didn't. Sure, he was tired enough after but the focus, the adrenaline rush he'd been looking for, had never come. It wasn't until then that he realized how much he missed the Sextant, missed being part of a team. He missed being on the line and getting slammed by so many orders that any minute they were going to be in the weeds. He missed clawing his way back through sheer bloody-minded determination, adrenaline pumping, hands flying, heart going overtime. He missed it. The kitchen at Pommes de Terre Vegas wasn't the same. It didn't feel right.

Neither did sitting in one of the casino's many plush bars afterward. There was none of the buzz of anticipation that had always hit him when he'd walked into a club in Manhattan, that feeling that something was about to happen. He felt only restless and bored. He didn't particularly want to be there, he realized as he sat at the bar.

He ordered scotch only because he wanted to be alone at his condo even less.

"Having a good night?" She was blond and beautiful, dressed in a scrap of a skirt that matched the glossy red of her lips. She slid onto the bar stool next to him with a look of frank female appreciation.

"Sure," he answered automatically. "You?"

"All right. There's only so much casino time I can take. My girlfriend's playing blackjack. I figured I'd take a break. How about you?"

He was supposed to be taking a break, too, and she was the kind of woman who'd always been his type. Why, then, did it feel like work to come up with a reply? "Me? Just stopping off on my way home."

"Oh yeah? Do you work here?"

"In the kitchen," he answered, already sorry he'd let himself get drawn into the conversation. Because she was studying him. Any moment it would hit, the journey of speculation to recognition to excitement.

She straightened. "Oh my God. You're that guy. The chef. I saw you on *Good Morning America*. You have a funny name, Damien somebody, right?"

And for the life of him he couldn't figure out why he was tempted to lie. "Damon," he said, taking a swallow of his scotch.

"Damon. Nice to meet you, Damon. I'm Leslie." She held out her hand, clasped his just a little too long. Her blue eyes gleamed. "So what does the name Damon mean? Are you a devil?"

Cady would have probably said so, he reflected. Then again, Cady hadn't given a damn for his celebrity. If anything, it had worked against him, as far as she was concerned. "Nope, not a devil. Just a guy."

"You look a little devilish to me," she said.

Her leg was pressed against his, her mouth was ripe. She was gorgeous and sexy and available.

And he had absolutely no interest in her at all. No arousal, even though her eyes told him he'd only to ask. But they were the wrong color eyes. They were the wrong color eyes and her makeup was too glossy and she didn't smell like apples and she was—

Not Cady.

The thought echoed through him. It was as simple as that, he realized, setting his glass down. It wasn't that his taste in women had changed, it was that Cady was the woman he wanted. Challenging, yes. Infuriating, almost certainly. Exciting, always. And generous and loyal and kind.

And he'd walked away from her.

What in the name of God had he been thinking?

Out in the casino there was a sudden cacophony of bells and sirens and shouts.

Leslie clutched his arm. "Someone's lucked out."

He'd lucked out back in Maine; he just hadn't realized it. He'd been so busy grabbing that brass ring Cady had talked about that he'd overlooked the pure gold right in front of him.

And suddenly, like a puzzle piece dropping into place, he realized the truth: he loved her. How had he missed that? How had he thought he could ever really walk away?

And not just from Cady, from the Compass Rose, the Sextant, the sense of home. The sense of family. He belonged in Grace Harbor. He belonged with her.

So what the hell was he doing sitting in a bar in Las Vegas?

"Excuse me." He picked Leslie's hand off his arm and rose.

She frowned. "Where are you going?"

He turned to look at her and he could feel the grin spread over his face. "The airport."

* * *

"You spend fifteen bucks for a lobster and you're putting Tabasco on it?" Tania asked.

Cady paused, bottle in the air. "I like Tabasco on lobster." She started shaking again.

"The Tabasco is for the steamers. The lobster gets the butter."

"The butter goes on the corn. Along with the Tabasco."

"I don't know why I take you anywhere," Tania muttered.

Cady just smiled. It was an old debate. They sat on the deck at Spiny's, a beachfront restaurant outside of Ogunquit, eating Sunday brunch in what had long been their ritual.

Or almost ritual.

For four weeks, she'd missed brunches with Tania. For four weeks, her Sundays had belonged to Damon and sheer happiness. Now, he was gone. Now, she was free for brunch again. And however much she ached, there was a comfort in the tradition that helped.

"You know, don't take this wrong but it's nice to be doing this again," Tania said, almost as though she'd known what Cady was thinking.

Cady looked out at the water. "I know I disappeared for a while. I'm sorry. Sometimes you've got to take advantage of the time you've got."

"I know." Tania took a drink of her mimosa. "So how are you doing?"

"I'm getting through," Cady said. It was, perhaps, the fairest assessment she could give. She'd endured almost four weeks so far. The days still crawled, but mornings no longer featured that unbearable moment of surfacing to realize that Damon was gone. The ache remained but she'd grown accustomed to it. And if she still wondered every hour on the hour where he was, what he was doing, well, time eventually would take care of that, too.

"Have you heard from him?" Tania asked.

Cady shook her head. "I didn't expect to. I'm sure he's off doing his thing, making a big success of himself."

"One of the women I do hair for saw him on the morning show a couple of weeks ago. Just raved about watching him cook and how she couldn't believe he was from Maine."

Cady raised her eyebrows. "From Maine?"

"Once down east, always down east."

"Not Damon. He's not down east anymore." As a joke, it didn't fly. There was a little too much misery hidden beneath.

Tania played with her water glass. "So he never asked you to go with him?"

"I think he knew it wasn't an option."

"Would you have gone if he'd asked?"

Cady gave a humorless laugh. "Oh, right, me in Vegas? I can just see it now. Fancy parties, VIP lounges, all-night gambling. Sequined dresses and high heels. Sounds like my kind of life."

"Would you have gone?"

"My life is here, Tania, you know that," she returned impatiently. "This patch of coast. My family, my job, my friends, my history, everything. This is what I'm about."

"Would you have gone?" Tania asked again.

Cady looked out at the water, staring at the horizon for long moments, watching a ship box the compass. "If he'd asked me," she said softly, "I would have gone anywhere with him."

He was very likely out of his mind, Damon thought as he headed down I-95 toward Grace Harbor. What guy quit a mid-six-figure job to go back to an opening that might not even exist? What guy would leave the biggest opportunity of his life to go back to a woman who'd told him to get lost? And who might very likely still feel that way?

Then again, what guy moved away from a place and never bothered to break his lease? It wasn't as if he'd been making the best decisions of late. He'd meant to do something about the rental house in Grace Harbor. The weeks had slid by and he'd put it off, telling himself he was too busy, telling himself that the rent was paid up to the end of the month and there would be time to come back out and close things up. But deep down, he knew that wasn't it.

He hadn't quite been able to make himself let it go.

Maybe somehow he'd known he was going to come back, he thought as he stopped his rental car outside her apartment. Or hoped. Which made him crazy for ever leaving to begin with. He should have known. Cady had.

And now all he wanted to do was make it right.

There was no answer to his knock on her door. For a moment, he stood, wondering. It was unlikely that she'd be working on a Sunday. He wasn't sure where else to try.

He stared at the featureless wood. He'd accused her of not knowing him at all, but he realized as he walked back to his car that he knew far too little of her. Their time together had consisted of Sundays and of stolen hours and minutes spread through the week. It wasn't a normal life he led. There wasn't much to offer her.

Moodily, he drove to the house he'd rented. The night before, it had all seemed simple: find her and tell her how he felt. On the red-eye back, he'd been sure that everything else would come together. But could it? Wouldn't a woman like Cady, so close with her family, want more than a life stolen in bits and pieces?

He walked into the house and he could feel her all around. They'd made love in every room, he remembered, and need for her arrowed through him. It was all right, he told himself. They would be together again. He'd make it work no matter what it took.

The house was hot, the air stale after a month of being closed in. He headed over to the slider, to open the place up.

And saw her.

She was bent over the vegetable beds in shorts and a T-shirt. Her hair glinted bright in the sun. Her truck was parked nearby with tools propped against it. And she was working on the garden. Their garden.

The plants had taken off, he saw in amazement. Neat rows of lettuce and herbs marched across the beds. The corn was a good foot tall. She'd tended it, he realized, staring at the pristine, weed-free soil, the lush green leaves, the carefully staked peppers and tomatoes. It wasn't hers. She'd thought he was gone for good, and yet she'd returned day after day to tend to it.

He was out the door before he even realized he'd opened the latch.

She should have brought a hat, Cady thought, taking off her gloves to turn up her music. Sun and mimosas were a bad combination. But it had been a spur-of-the-moment decision to come. The conversation at brunch had made her miss Damon fiercely and she hadn't been able to bear the idea of sitting around her apartment. And so she'd come to work in the garden. Somehow, even though the reminder of him hurt, she felt an obscure comfort in working the ground they'd tilled together. She felt connected to him in some way.

When he'd gone, she'd expected the landlord to let the place again. No new tenants had materialized, though, so she'd just kept coming over, driving her truck around back to unload whatever she needed. Soon, she wouldn't be bringing it back to drop off tools and supplies; she'd be bringing it back to take away the harvest.

And one day, the plants would all die, the last tangible reminder of a time that had been a miraculous surprise, a wonderful gift, a precious time that would never come again.

She pressed the heels of her hands against her eyelids until patterns of orange and black and green appeared.

"You've been busy."

People could jump out of their skin, she discovered. It wasn't just a saying. And when she whirled around, she was stunned to find Damon standing there.

She had to be dreaming, Cady thought wildly, or drunk or delusional. Adrenaline made her shaky. She couldn't seem to get her breath. In her ears, Alison Krauss and Robert Plant sang about being gone, gone, gone but he was there before her looking rumpled and unshaven and she wanted to weep at how good it felt.

Instead, she stood, wiping her hands off on her shorts. "I, uh, was just stopping by."

"It looks like you've been doing that a lot," he said, turning to survey the tidy beds.

"I couldn't just let it go. I couldn't let them burn up." She hadn't quite been able to abandon that last reminder of something they'd planted together. Her mouth was dry. "What are you doing here?"

"I couldn't let go, either," he said softly.

"What happened to the job?"

"It didn't work."

"The restaurants?" She stared.

He gave a short laugh. "No, the restaurants are doing great. I'm the one who wasn't. Cady, I screwed up. I went carting off after that job because that's what I thought I wanted. It's always been my big dream. But sometimes your dreams change on you before you have a chance to catch up." He met her gaze. "My dream's here now, with you."

She wanted to sink into the warmth in his eyes. She wanted to find herself back in his arms. Instead, she made herself keep her distance. After all, she'd forgotten once before. "So you're back?"

"I sat out there and all I could think about was how it didn't feel right, how it wasn't what I thought it would be. Because it wasn't like here, I figured out. All I did was miss this place. And all I did was think about you and miss you. So yeah, I'm back."

"For now." She raised her chin.

"For good."

"What does that mean?" she asked with a thread of desperation. "How do I know that's not going to change in a month or a year when you decide you're bored with this? When the party machine gets cranked up? When Jack comes to town with a new offer?"

"Trust me, he won't." Damon smiled faintly. "You're what I want. I know that. A life with you, a life here in Grace Harbor, planting gardens, cooking at the restaurant, making a home."

"Don't play me, Damon." Her voice shook. "What happened with us…I let you in like I've never let anyone in before. Ever. And it about killed me when you left. I don't think I could go through that again, so if this is some kind of a lark with you, something you're doing to kill time, go away. I don't want you."

He reached out and took her hands in his. "What about if it's not a lark? What about if I want to be with you for the rest of my life? I love you, Cady. I realized it last night. And I know that being involved with someone in the restaurant business sucks," he hurried on while her mouth was still gaping open. "The hours are terrible. But I swear to you, I'll make it work. If I can still come back to the Sextant, Roman and I can get things rolling to where we'll both have lives. And I want to spend mine with you. Believe me," he whispered. "Believe in me."

She stared at him in wonder for a long moment. And launched herself into his arms. "Oh God." She half laughed, half choked. "I love you so much. I knew the weekend of my dad's party. I thought I was going to die without you."

"Live with me, instead. Marry me, Cady. Grow gardens with me, a family. Grow old with me."

It couldn't be real, she thought to herself. She couldn't be hearing the words but it was and she was, and his arms were warm around her. She gazed into his eyes. "Do you mean it?"

"Yes."

"Really?"

"Yes."

"Because, well, if we're going to be growing things, there's an ancient fertility rite I've been told about." She traced a finger over his lips.

He squeezed her tighter and pressed his mouth to hers. "I know just the one."

* * * * *

The Colton family is back!
Enjoy a sneak preview of
COLTON'S SECRET SERVICE
by Marie Ferrarella,
part of
THE COLTONS: FAMILY FIRST *miniseries.*

Available from Silhouette Romantic Suspense
in September 2008.

He cautioned himself to be leery. He was human and he'd been conned before. But never by anyone nearly so attractive. Never by anyone he'd felt so attracted to.

In her defense, Nick supposed that Georgie could actually be telling him the truth. That she was a victim in all this. He had his people back in California checking her out, to make sure she was who she said she was and had, as she claimed, not even been near a computer but on the road these last few months that the threats had been made.

In the meantime, he was doing his own checking out. Up close and exceedingly personal. So personal he could feel his blood stirring.

It had been a long time since he'd thought of himself as anything other than a law enforcement agent of one type or other. But Georgeann Grady made him remember that beneath the oaths he had taken and his devotion to duty, there beat the heart of a man.

A man who'd been far too long without the touch of a woman.

He watched as the light from the fireplace caressed the outline of Georgie's small, trim, jeans-clad body as she moved about the rustic living room that could have easily come off the set of a Hollywood Western. Except that it was genuine.

As genuine as she claimed to be?

Something inside of him hoped so.

He wasn't supposed to be taking sides. His only interest in being here was to guarantee Senator Joe Colton's safety as the latter continued to make his bid for the presidency. Everything else was supposed to be secondary, but, Nick had to silently admit, that was just a wee bit hard to remember right now.

Earlier, before she'd put her precocious handful of a daughter to bed, Georgie had fed his appetite by whipping up some kind of a delicious concoction out of the vegetables she'd pulled from her garden. Vegetables that, by all rights, should have been withered and dried. She'd mentioned that a friend came by on occasion to weed and tend it. Still, it surprised him that somehow she'd managed to make something mouthwatering out of it.

Almost as mouthwatering as she looked to him right at this moment.

Again, he was reminded of the appetite that hadn't been fed, hadn't been satisfied.

And wasn't going to be, Nick sternly told himself. At least not now. Maybe later, when things took on a more definite shape and all the questions in his head were answered to his satisfaction, there would be time to explore this feeling. This woman. But not now.

Damn it.

"Sorry about the lack of light," Georgie said, breaking into his train of thought as she turned around to face him. If she noticed the way he was looking at her, she gave no indication. "But I don't see a point in paying for electricity if I'm not going to be here. Besides, Emmie really enjoys camping out. She likes roughing it."

"And you?" Nick asked, moving closer to her, so close that a whisper would have trouble fitting in. "What do you like?"

The very breath stopped in Georgie's throat as she looked up at him.

"I think you've got a fair shot of guessing that one," she told him softly.

* * * * *

Be sure to look for
COLTON'S SECRET SERVICE
and the other following titles from
THE COLTONS: FAMILY FIRST *miniseries:*

RANCHER'S REDEMPTION
by Beth Cornelison
THE SHERIFF'S AMNESIAC BRIDE
by Linda Conrad
SOLDIER'S SECRET CHILD
by Caridad Piñeiro
BABY'S WATCH
by Justine Davis
A HERO OF HER OWN
by Carla Cassidy

Romantic
SUSPENSE

Sparked by Danger, Fueled by Passion.

The Coltons Are Back!

Marie Ferrarella
Colton's Secret Service

The Coltons: Family First

On a mission to protect a senator, Secret Service agent
Nick Sheffield tracks down a threatening message only
to discover Georgie Gradie Colton, a rodeo-riding single
mom, who insists on her innocence. Nick is instantly
taken with the feisty redhead, but vows not to let his
feelings interfere with his mission. Now he must figure
out if this woman is conning him or if he can trust her
and the passion they share....

Available September wherever books are sold.

**Look for upcoming Colton titles
from Silhouette Romantic Suspense:**

RANCHER'S REDEMPTION by Beth Cornelison, Available October
THE SHERIFF'S AMNESIAC BRIDE by Linda Conrad, Available November
SOLDIER'S SECRET CHILD by Caridad Piñeiro, Available December
BABY'S WATCH by Justine Davis, Available January 2009
A HERO OF HER OWN by Carla Cassidy, Available February 2009

Visit Silhouette Books at www.eHarlequin.com   SRS27598

Silhouette®

SPECIAL EDITION

HEART OF STONE
by
DIANA PALMER

On sale September.

SAVE $1.⁰⁰ OFF

**the Silhouette Special Edition® novel
HEART OF STONE on sale
September 2008, when you purchase
2 Silhouette Special Edition® books.**

*Available wherever books are sold, including most
bookstores, supermarkets, drugstores and discount stores.*

Coupon expires December 31, 2008. Redeemable at participating
retail outlets in the U.S. only. Limit one coupon per customer.

U.S. RETAILERS: Harlequin Enterprises Limited will pay the face value of this coupon plus
8¢ if submitted by customer for this specified product only. Any other use constitutes fraud.
Coupon is nonassignable. Void if taxed, prohibited or restricted by law. Consumer must pay
any government taxes. Void if copied. For reimbursement submit coupons and proof of sales
directly to Harlequin Enterprises Limited, P.O. Box 880478, El Paso, TX 88588-0478, U.S.A.
Cash value 1/100 cents. Limit one coupon per customer. Valid in the U.S. only.

5 65373 00076 2   (8100) 0 11556   SSECPNUS0808

REQUEST YOUR FREE BOOKS!
2 FREE NOVELS PLUS 2 FREE GIFTS!

SPECIAL EDITION®
Life, Love and Family!

YES! Please send me 2 FREE Silhouette Special Edition® novels and my 2 FREE gifts (gifts are worth about $10). After receiving them, if I don't wish to receive any more books, I can return the shipping statement marked "cancel." If I don't cancel, I will receive 6 brand-new novels every month and be billed just $4.24 per book in the U.S. or $4.99 per book in Canada, plus 25¢ shipping and handling per book and applicable taxes, if any*. That's a savings of at least 15% off the cover price! I understand that accepting the 2 free books and gifts places me under no obligation to buy anything. I can always return a shipment and cancel at any time. Even if I never buy another book from Silhouette, the two free books and gifts are mine to keep forever.

235 SDN EEYU 335 SDN EEY6

Name   (PLEASE PRINT)

Address   Apt. #

City   State/Prov.   Zip/Postal Code

Signature (if under 18, a parent or guardian must sign)

Mail to the Silhouette Reader Service:
IN U.S.A.: P.O. Box 1867, Buffalo, NY 14240-1867
IN CANADA: P.O. Box 609, Fort Erie, Ontario L2A 5X3

Not valid to current subscribers of Silhouette Special Edition books.

Want to try two free books from another line?
Call 1-800-873-8635 or visit www.morefreebooks.com.

* Terms and prices subject to change without notice. N.Y. residents add applicable sales tax. Canadian residents will be charged applicable provincial taxes and GST. Offer not valid in Quebec. This offer is limited to one order per household. All orders subject to approval. Credit or debit balances in a customer's account(s) may be offset by any other outstanding balance owed by or to the customer. Please allow 4 to 6 weeks for delivery. Offer available while quantities last.

Your Privacy: Silhouette is committed to protecting your privacy. Our Privacy Policy is available online at www.eHarlequin.com or upon request from the Reader Service. From time to time we make our lists of customers available to reputable third parties who may have a product or service of interest to you. If you would prefer we not share your name and address, please check here. ☐

SSE08R

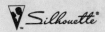

SPECIAL EDITION

HEART OF STONE

by

DIANA PALMER

On sale September.

SAVE $1.⁰⁰ OFF

the Silhouette Special Edition® novel
HEART OF STONE on sale
September 2008, when you purchase
2 Silhouette Special Edition® books.

*Available wherever books are sold, including most
bookstores, supermarkets, drugstores and discount stores.*

Coupon expires December 31, 2008. Redeemable at participating
retail outlets in Canada only. Limit one coupon per customer.

52608458

SSECPNCDN0808

COMING NEXT MONTH